Paul Hamilton Hayne

The Mountain of the Lovers

With Poems of Nature and Tradition

Paul Hamilton Hayne

The Mountain of the Lovers
With Poems of Nature and Tradition

ISBN/EAN: 9783744769990

Printed in Europe, USA, Canada, Australia, Japan

Cover: Foto ©Andreas Hilbeck / pixelio.de

More available books at **www.hansebooks.com**

THE MOUNTAIN OF THE LOVERS;

WITH

POEMS OF NATURE AND TRADITION.

BY

PAUL H. HAYNE.

NEW YORK:

E. J. HALE & SON, PUBLISHERS,
MURRAY STREET.
1875.

RUSSELL BROTHERS,
Printers, Electrotypers and Stereotypers,
17, 19, 21 and 23 Rose Street, New York.

Dedication.

TO

MARGARET J. PRESTON,

OF VIRGINIA.

Mine eyes have never gazed in thine,
Our hands are strangers; yet divine
The deathless sympathy which binds
    Our hearts and minds!

Thou singest along the mountain side;
Thy golden songs are justified
By the rich music of their flow;
    I sing below,

Where the lone pine-land airs are stirred
By notes of thrush and mocking bird;—
The heights befit thy loftier strain;
    Mine courts the plain.

DEDICATION.

And now, with joyous sylvan things
All round me, 'mid the flash of wings,
The rivulet's lapse, the breeze's play,
    On this bright day,

Flushed like a Dryad's tender face
With early spring-time's happiest grace,
This day of soft harmonious hours,
    Made sweet with flowers,

My lowland Muse is blithe to send
Fair greeting to her mountain friend,
And—yearning more for love than praise—
    These wild-wood lays!

CONTENTS.

The Mountain of the Lovers.

[The most important feature in the landscape of this poem the old Chronicler persists in designating as a mountain of "steep" and "terrible"
ascent ; but that it could not have been a mountain, and, despite certain ob-
stacles which made it dangerous for men on horseback, it might not even
have been a *very* "terrible" hill, is shown by the fact, that among the
crowd who reached the summit soon after the catastrophe, were "old men,"
whom the excitement of the time and scene would hardly have sufficed to
bear safely up were the Chronicler's expressions to be *literally* accepted. To
any man loaded as Oswald was, the ascent of a comparatively moderate
height would prove a fearful trial ; but in his case the atrocious cruelty of
the experiment, and the life and death issues involved, became so closely
associated in the spectators' minds with the *material* scene of the tragedy,
that the latter was not unnaturally beheld through the magnifying medium
of pity and terror. Thus the hill was elevated into a mountain ! The old
Chronicler celebrates it as such. We follow the old Chronicler—to the
death !]

I.

Love scorns degrees ! the low he lifteth high,
The high he draweth down to that fair plain
Whereon, in his divine equality,
Two loving hearts may meet, nor meet in vain ;
'Gainst such sweet levelling Custom cries amain,
But o'er its harshest utterance one bland sigh,
Breathed passion-wise, doth mount victorious still,
For Love, earth's lord, must have his lordly will.

II.

But ah! this sovereign will oft works at last
The deadliest bane, as happed erewhile to her,
Earl Godolf's daughter, many a century past:
She loved her father's low born Forester,
About whose manful grace did breathe and stir
So clear a radiance by soul-virtues cast,
He moved untouched of social blight or ban—
Nature's serene, true-hearted gentleman.

III.

Yet she alone of all the household saw
That lofty soul beneath his serf's attire;
But of the ruthless Earl so great her awe,
Close, close she kept her spirit's veiled desire,
Nor outward shone one spark of hidden fire.
Too well she knew to what stern feudal law
She and her hapless Love perforce must yield,
If once this tender secret were revealed.

IV.

Yea! even by Oswald's self her covert flame
Undreamed of burned; proud stood she, coldly fair,
When, to report of woodcraft lore, he came
To the Earl's hall, and she was lingering there.

"Cold heart!" thought he; "who, 'midst her liege-
    men, dare
Play as I played with death a desperate game
For her sweet sake? and yet, alas! and yet,
She scorns the service and disowns the debt."

V.

For sooth it was that one keen winter's night,
While slowly journeying homeward through a wood
Whose every deepest copse in moonshine bright
Glimmered from hoary trunk to frost-tipped bud,
On sire and child there burst a cry of blood,
Followed by hurrying feet, and the dread sight
Of scores of grey-skinned brutes—a direful pack
Of wolves half starved that yelled along their track.

VI.

In vain his frantic team Earl Godolf smote,
With blended prayer and curse; nigh doom were
    they,
Riders and steeds, for now each ravening throat
Yawned like a foul tomb. On the bounding sleigh
The fierce horde gained, when from the silvery-gray,
Cold-branchèd glades outrang a bugle note,
With next a bowstring's twang, an arrowy whirr,
As shaft on shaft the keen-eyed Forester

VII.

Launched on the foe, each hurtling shaft a fate.
Then Oswald, 'twixt pursuers and pursued
Leapt, sword in hand, his eyes of fiery hate
Fixed on the baffled horde, whose doubtful mood
Changed to quick fear, they scoured adown the wood,
Their long gaunt lines, in fiend-like, vanquished state,
Fading with flash of blood-red orbs from far,
Till the last vanished like a baleful star!

VIII.

Now, by the mass! abrupt and brief, I ween,
The rude Earl's thanks for rescued limbs and life;
But not so graceless proved the fair Catrine,
As glancing backward to the field of strife
She flashed a smile with cordial meaning rife,
Which struck our sylvan hero (who did lean,
Pale, on his bow,) as 'twere the piercing gleam
Of some strange, sudden, half bewildering dream.

IX.

Alack! the dream waxed not, but seemed to wane,
As if a cloudless sun but late arisen,
Back journeying, passed across the ethereal plain,
And the fresh dawn it brought, died out in heaven;

For from that eve no subtlest signs were given—
As erst we said—that passion's blissful pain
Touched the maid's heart, or that her days were
    caught
In those fine meshes woven by love for thought.

X.

In Britain dwelt Earl Godolf, nigh the bounds
Of the Welsh marches; a wild rover he
·In his hot youth, inured to strife and wounds
Through many a foray fierce by land and sea;
But, after years of bright tranquillity—
Years linked to love through pleasure's peaceful
    rounds
So gently lapsed, the unmailed warrior's hand
Forgot almost the use of spear or brand.

XI.

A bride erewhile won by his dauntless blade
In a great sea fight—where his arm had slain
Some half score foemen—wan and half afraid,
Homeward he brought, whose every delicate vein
Pulsed the rich blood and tropic warmth of Spain;
But when pure wifehood crowned the noble maid,
Heart-fruits for him his beauteous lady bore,
Of whose strange sweets he had not dreamed before.

XII.

She strove his nature's ruggedness to smooth,
And in his bosom dropped a fruitful germ
Of those mild virtues given our lives to soothe,
And change their gusty solitude to warm
Beneficent calm,—divinest after storm.
Within him flowered a pallid grace of ruth,
Nor oft, as once, o'er bleeding breasts he trod
Straight to his purpose, blind to Law and God.

XIII.

And in fair fullness of the ripened time,
Still gentler grew his dark, war furrowed mien;
He quaffed the sunshine of a fairy clime,
Love charmed, hope gladdened; when, to crown the
    scene
Of transient bliss, there smiled a new Catrine—
The loveliest babe e'er lulled by mother's rhyme—
Whose tiny fingers o'er her heart strings played,
Making ineffable music where they strayed.

XIV.

Woe worth the end! for, though the infant thrived,
Slowly the hapless mother pined away;
Love to the last in pleading eyes survived—
Those fond, fond eyes doomed to the churchyard
    clay,

Coffined, and shut from all blithe sights of day;
But Christ! in thee her stainless spirit lived,
Whose memory—a white star—should evermore
O'er her Lord's paths have beamed to keep them
    pure.

X V.

Nathless, some souls there are by cruel loss
Stung, as with scourge of scorpions, to despair;
These will not seek the Christ, nor clasp His Cross,
But, groping vaguely through sulphureous air,
Strike hands with Satan, in the murky glare
Of furious hell, whose billows rage and toss
About their tortured being, urged to curse
That mystic WILL which rules the universe.

XVI.

Yea, such the Earl's; no cooling dew did fall
To heal his wound; 'gainst heaven and earth he
    turned,
Girt to his sense with one vast funeral pall;
And the sore heart within him writhed and burned
With baffled hope, and pain that madly yearned,
Vainly and madly, for dear love's recall.
No light o'ershone grief's ocean drear and black,
The while old passions thronged tumultuous back.

XVII.

So, his last state was worse than e'en his first;
Murder and Rapine, pitiless Greed, and Ire
Raged wheresoe'er his Raven banner burst,
'Mid shrieks and wails, and hollow roar of fire,
Which lapped the household porch and crackling
    byre;
He seemed demoniac in his aims accurst,
Wrath in his soul, and on his brow the sign
Of hell—a human scourge by power divine

XVIII.

For some mysterious end permitted still—
As many an evil thing our God allows
To range the world, and work its dreadful will,
Whether in form of chiefs, with laureled brows,
Or spies and traitors in the good man's house;
Or, it may be, some slow, infectious Ill,
Untraced, and rising like a mist defiled
With poisonous odors on a lonely wild,

XIX.

Albeit no marsh is near, or steamy fen.
More monstrous year by year Earl Godolf's deeds
Flared in hell's livery on the eyes of men;
All growths of transient goodness checked by weeds,

Sin-bred; and, ah! *one* angel's bosom bleeds
To know she may not meet her love again;
And even the vales immortal seemed less sweet,
Because too pure for his crime-cumbered feet.

XX.

But, weal or woe, the world rolls blindly on,
While nature's charm, in child, and bird, and flower,
Works its rare marvels 'neath the noonday sun,
And the still stars in midnight's slumberous hour.
And so a human bud, through beam and shower,
Glad play, and easeful sleep—the orphaned one,
The beauteous babe—a sour old beldame's care,
Upflowered at length a matchless maid, and fair.

XXI.

Most fair to all but him to whom she owed
Her life and place in this bewildering world;
For he, a changed man since that hour which showed
His wife's worn form in earthly cerements furled,
Cold scorn had launched, or captious passion hurled
At this sole offspring of his lone abode,
Till grown, alas! too early grave and wise,
She viewed her sire, in turn, with loveless eyes.

XXII.

Still in benignant arms did Nature fold
Her favored child, and on her richly showered
All gifts of beauty; with long hair of gold
And lucid, languid eyes the maid she dowered,
And her enticing loveliness empowered
With charms to melt the wintriest temper's cold—
Charms wrought of sunrise warmth, and twilight
     balm,
Passion's deep glow, and Pity's saint-like calm.

XXIII.

Tall, lithe, and yielding as a young bay tree
Her perfect form; but 'neath its lissom grace
There lurked a latent strength keen eyes could see,
Drawn from her father's undegenerate race;
The dazzling fairness of her Saxon face,
Contrasted with the dark eyes' witchery,
Shone with such light as Northern noondays wake
Through the clear shadows of a mountain lake.

XXIV.

Her full blown flower of beauty lured 'ere long
Unnumbered suitors round her; these declare
Boldest report hath done the virgin wrong,
And past all power of words they deem her fair;

The kingdom's princeliest youth besiege her ear
And heart with ardent vows and amorous song;
Love, rank and wealth their splendid beams combine,
She the rare orb about whose path they shine.

XXV.

Still would she wed with none, till rudely pressed
To the last boundary of her patience sweet;
No more she struggled in a yearning breast
To hide her passion, howsoe'er unmeet
For one high placed as she; her fervent feet
Oft bore her now where woodland flowers caressed
The grand old oaks, beneath whose sheltering
    boughs
The lovers mused, or, whispering, breathed their
    vows.

XXVI.

But ere to such sweet pass their fates had led,
Or ere her thought unbosomed utterly,
To the 'rapt youth, in tremulous tones, she said,
" *I love thee,*" through full many a fine degree
Of feeling, touched by sad uncertainty,
That truth they neared, which, like a bird o'erhead,
Still faltering flew, till borne through shade and sun,
It nestled warm in two hearts made as one!

XXVII.

The truth, the fond conviction that all earth
Was less than naught—a mote, a vanishing gleam,
Matched with the glow of that transcendant birth
Of love which wrapped them in his happiest dream;
Entranced thus, shut in by beam on beam
Of glory, is it strange but trivial worth
Their dazzled minds in transient doubts should see
Which sometimes crossed their keen felicity?

XXVIII.

Their love awhile, like some smooth rivulet borne
Through drooping umbrage of a lonely dell,
By clouds unvisited, by storms untorn,
Passed, rippling music; like a magic bell
Outrung by spirit-hands invisible,
Each tender hour of meeting, eve or morn,
Above them stole in rhythmic sweetness, blent
With rare fruition of supreme content.

XXIX.

But in the sunset tide of one calm day,
When, all unconscious, at the place of tryst,
Beyond their wont they lingered; with dismay
They saw, begirt by gold and amethyst

Of that rich time, gigantic in the mist
Of shimmering splendor, which did flash and play
About his form, and o'er his visage dire,
The wrathful Earl, midmost the sunset fire.

XXX.

No word he uttered, but his falchion drew,
Red with the slain boar's blood, and pointed grim
Where 'gainst the eastern heavens' slow-deepening
    blue
Uprose his castle turrets, tall and dim.
The maid's eyes close; she feels each nerveless limb
Sink nigh to swooning; but, heart-brave and true,
Clings to her Love, while from pale lips a sigh
Doth faintly fall, which means *" with him I die !"*

XXXI.

Gravely advancing, the Earl's stalwart hand
Rests on her shuddering shoulder; one quick glance,
Haughty and high, rife with severe command,
On the 'mazed Woodsman doth he dart askance,
Who doubtful bides, as one half roused from trance,
Striving to know on what new ground his stand
Thenceforth shall be; or, if life's priceless ALL,
Put to the test just then, must rise or fall.

XXXII.

Fate-wrought the issue! for as Oswald waits
Biding his time to smite, or else retreat,
With the maid's hand his own Earl Godolf mates,
And from the wood they pass with footsteps fleet;
One tearful, backward look vouchsafed his sweet,
Just as the castle gates—those iron gates,
Heavy and stern, like Death's—were closed between
His burning vision and the lost Catrine.

XXXIII.

To heaven he raises wild, despairing eyes,
But heaven responds not; then to earth returns
His baffled gaze from ranging the cold skies,
And earth but seems a place for burial urns;
In sooth, the whole creation mutely spurns
His prayer for aid; alas! what kind replies
Can woeful man from fair, dumb Nature draw
Locked in the grasp of adamantine Law?

XXXIV.

Three morns thereafter, in the market place
Of the small town, from Godolf's castle wall
Distant, it might be, some twelve furlongs' space,
Came, grandly robed, our Lord's high seneschal;

To all the lieges, with shrill trumpet call.
In name of his serene puissant grace
Godolf, the Earl; to all folk, bond or free,
With strident voice he read this foul decree:

XXXV.

" Whereas our virgin daughter, hight Catrine,
False to her noble race and lineage proud,
Hath owned her love for one of birth as mean
As any hind's who creeps among the crowd
Of common serfs, with cowering shoulders bowed—
Oswald by name—the whom ourselves have seen,
When least he deemed us nigh, his traitorous part
Press with hot wooing on the maiden's heart:

XXXVI.

" Let all men know hereby our will it is,
To-morrow morn their trial morn must be ;
Either the serf shall win, and call her his,
Or both shall taste such bitter misery
As even in dreams the boldest soul would flee ;
If lips unlicensed thus will meet and kiss,
Reason it seems that such unhallowed flame
Of love should end in agony and shame.

XXXVII.

"Therefore, the morrow morn shall view their doom
Accomplished; 'mid the ferns of Bolton Down,
Where Bolton Height doth catch the purpling
    bloom
Of early sunrise on his treeless crown,
We say to all—knight, burgher, squire and clown—
Just as the castle's morning bell shall boom
O'er the far hills, and brown moor's blossoming,
Come, and behold a yet undreamed-of thing.

XXXVIII.

"For then and there must Oswald bear aloft,
By his sole strength, unaided and alone,
The blameful maid, whose nature, grown too soft,
Durst thus betray our honor and her own;
Yet, if he gain the height, untamed, unthrown,
All hands applaud him, and all plumes be doffed;
While for ourselves, we vow they both shall fare
Unharmed beyond our realm—we reck not where."

XXXIX.

So, as decreed, the next morn, calm and clear,
Witnessed, in many a diverse mode conveyed,
A mixed and mighty concourse gathering near
The appointed height, some in rough frieze arrayed,

And some in gold; there blushed the downcast maid,
Urged to this cruel test, a passionate tear
Misting her view, as surged the living sea.
Behind her, his arms folded haughtily,

XL.

His comely head thrown back, his eyes on fire
With hot contempt, fixed on an arméd band
Which, stationed near him by the Earl's desire,
His every move o'erlooked, did Oswald stand,
Striving his rouséd anger to command,
And lift his clouded aspirations higher
Than thoughts revengeful. Hark! a deepening hum
On the crowd's verge—the trial hour has come!

XLI.

Divided, then, betwixt his ire and scorn,
Outspake the Earl, in tones of savage glee:
" Woodsman! essay thy task, for lo! the morn
Grows old, and I this wretched mummery
Would fain see ended."
     —With mien gravely free,
Clad in light garb, o'erwrought by hound and horn,
Oswald stood forth, nor quelled by frail alarms,
About the maiden clasped his reverent arms;

XLII.

And she, like some pure flower by May tide rain
Gracefully laden, turns her eyes apart
From the great throng, and, pierced by modest
    pain,
Veils her sweet face upon her lover's heart;
Whereat the youth is seen to thrill and start,
While o'er his own face, calm and pale but now,
Rush the deep crimson waves from chin to brow;

XLIII.

Then do they ebb away, and leave him white
As the vexed foam on ocean's stormy swell,
Yet cool and constant in his manful might
As some staunch rock 'gainst which the tides rebel
In useless rage, with hollow, billowy knell;
Meanwhile, advancing with sure steps and light,
He moves in measured wise to dare his fate
Beneath those looks of blended ruth and hate.

XLIV.

Stirred by his generous bravery, and the sight
Of such young lives—their love, hope, joyance set
On the hard mastery of yon terrible height,
Whose rugged slopes and sheer descent are wet

And slippery with the dews of dawning yet,
Through the dense rout, which swayed now left, now
    right,
Low, inarticulate murmurs faintly ran,
And one keen, quivering shock from man to man.

XLV.

The watchful matrons sob, the virgins weep
Full tears, but all unheeded, as with slow,
Sure footfalls still he mounts the hostile steep
On to a point where two great columns show
Their rounded heads, crowned by the morning glow.
His task half done, a sigh, long, grateful, deep,
Breaks from his heaving heart; secure he stands,
A sunbeam glimmering on his claspéd hands,

XLVI.

And the glad lustre of his wind-swept locks
More radiant made thereby; his tall form towers
'Gainst the dark background, piled with rocks on
    rocks
Precipitous, whose grim, gaunt visage lowers,
As if in league they were—like Titan powers
Victorious long o'er storms and earthquake shocks—
To cast mute scorn on him whose doubtful path
Leads near the threatening shadows of their wrath.

XLVII.

From the charmed crowd then rose an easeful breath,
Lightening the dense air; but, 'midst doubt and
    bale,
Raves the wild Earl, reckless of life or death,
If so his tyrannous purpose could prevail;
For, almost mad, he smites his gloves of mail,
Goading with frenzied heel the steed beneath
His barbarous rule; in reason's fierce eclipse,
A blood red foam burns on his writhing lips.

XLVIII.

Meanwhile, brief space for needful respite given,
With quickened pace, onward and upward still,
And fanned by freshening gales, as nearer heaven
He climbs o'er granite passways of the hill,
Oswald ascends, untamed of strength or will,
Striving, as ne'er before had mortal striven,
Boldly to win, and proudly wear as his,
The prize he bore of that bright, breathing Bliss.

XLIX.

Two thirds, two thirds and more, of that last half
Of his fell journey had he stoutly won;
And now he pauses the cool breeze to quaff,
And feel the royal heartening of the sun

Nerving his soul for what must yet be done,
When with a gentle, quivering, flutelike laugh,
Holding a sob, the maiden rose and kissed
Her hero's lips, sought through a tremulous mist

L.

Of love and pride!   The on-lookers, ranged afar,
Saw, and more boldly blessed them; all are moved
To trust that theirs may prove the fortunate star
Fate brightly kindles for young lives beloved:
" His truth and valor hath he nobly proved;
How brave, how constant both these lovers are!
Sooth! the sweet heavens seem with them."   Thus,
    full voiced,
Yet with some lingering doubts, the folk rejoiced.

LI.

Alas! for false forecasting, and surmise!
Though small the space betwixt him and his goal,
Oswald doth stagger now in feeblest wise,
And like some drunken carl, with heave and roll,
Blindly he staggers in his lost control
Of sense, or power; and so, with anguished sighs,
Turned on his love—the goal in easy reach—
His yearning woe too deep for mortal speech.

LII.

Whereon the lady's arms are wildly raised,
Perchance in prayer, perchance with pitying aim
His strain to ease, when lo ! (dear Christ be praised !)
It seemed new strength, fresh courage o'er him came,
And through his spirit rushed a glorious flame,
At which the crowd stood moveless, dumb, amazed,
For, like a god, with swift, resistless tread,
He strides to clasp the near goal o'er his head.

LIII.

A savage cliff of beetling brow it was,
Midmost the summit of the lowering height,
Rooted amongst low shrubs and sun dried grass,
And reared in blackness, like a cloud of night,
On whose dull breast no beacon star is bright.
Thitherward, from cold terrors of the pass
Well nigh of death, the hero speeds amain,
Nor seems his matchless labor wrought in vain.

LIV.

Yea; for a single rood's length oversped,
And victory crowns him ! God ! how still the crowd,
Once rife with voices ! silent as the dead
Lodged in their earthly crypt and mouldering
    shroud ;

But suddenly a great cry mounted loud
And shrill above them, as in ruthful dread,
They saw the lovers, linked in close embrace,
Fall headlong down by that wild trysting place.

L V.

Then comes a quick revulsion, when the pain
Of fear and choking sympathy gone by,
Hope reappears—aye, joy and triumph reign—
For though supine on yonder height they lie,
Still, brow to brow, turned from the deepening sky,
'Tis but the faintness of the mighty strain—
Or so they dream—on o'erworked nerve and will,
Which leaves them moveless on the conquered hill.

L V I.

Spurring his courser, in vexed doubt and haste,
The Earl charged on the dangerous height, as
        though
Firm-trenched, defiant, 'mid the rock-strewn waste,
Glittered the spear points of his mortal foe;
The horse's hoof struck fire, hurling below
Huge stones and turf his goaded limbs displaced,
Till checked midway, his reckless rider found
He needs must climb afoot the treacherous ground.

LVII.

And next the throng had caught, and past him swept,
Clothed as he was in armor; a young knight
Headed the rout, whose feverish fingers crept
Oft to his sword hilt; on the topmost height,
Pausing with veilèd eyes, his gaze he kept
Fixed on the prostrate pair, o'er whom the light
Of broadening sunrise now was mixed with shade,
And still the knight's hand wandered round his
    blade.

LVIII.

Impatient, spleenful, struggling with the tide
Of common folk, who seemed to heed no more
His sullen passion and revengeful pride,
Than if just then he were the veriest boor,
The Earl at length with bent brows strode before
The mongrel horde, and unto Oswald cried:
" Rise, traitor, rise! by some foul, juggling sleight,
Through the fiend's help, thou hast attained the
    height:

LIX.

Part them, I say!" To whom in measured tone,
Measured and strange, the young knight answering
    said:

" Earl ! well I know thou wear'st for heart a stone,
Yet dar'st thou part these twain whom Death has
  wed,
No longer twain, but one?   Look ! overhead
The burning sun mounts to his noonday throne ;
But o'er the sun, as o'er this fateful sod,
Rules a great King, the King whose name is God !

LX.

" Deem'st thou for this day's work His wrath shall
  rest ?"
Whereon, low murmuring like a hive of bees,
With stifled groans and tears, the people pressed
Round the fair corpses—women on their knees
Embraced them—and old men—but dusky lees
Of feeling left—did touch them, and caressed
The maid's soft hair, the woodsman's noble face,
Praying, under breath, that Christ would grant them
  grace.

* * * * *

That mournful day had waned ; by sunset rose
A wailing wind from out the dim northeast ;
Which, as the shadows waxed at twilight's close
O'er mote and wood, to a shrill storm increased ;

But in his castle hall, with song and feast,
Varied full oft by ribald gibes and blows
Twixt ruffian guests in rage or maudlin play,
The wild night raved its awful hours away.

With not a pang at thought of her whose form
In pallid beauty lay unwatched and dead,
In a far turret chamber, where the storm,
Thundering each moment louder overhead,
Entered and shook the close-draped, sombre bed,
The barbarous sire with wine and wassail warm,
Lifting his cup 'mid brutal jest and jeer
Banned his pale daughter, slumbering on her bier.

Just as those impious words had taken flight,
In the red dusk beyond the torch's glare,
Stole a vague Shape that 'scaped the revellers' sight,
Slowly toward Earl Godolf, unaware
Even as the rest, what fateful foe drew near.
Muffled the Shape was, masked and black as night,
And now for one dread instant with raised sword
Stood hovering o'er the heedless banquet board.

And next with flashing motion fierce and fast,
Vengeance descended on that glittering blade ;
The amazed spectators started, dumb, aghast,
While at their feet the caitiff lord was laid,

His heart's blood trickling o'er the purple braid
(For thro' his heart the avenger's brand had passed),
And silver broidery of his gorgeous vest,
Drawn drop by drop from out his smitten breast.

The muffled Shape which as a cloud did rise
On the wild orgie, as a cloud departs;
Wan hands are swept across bewildered eyes,
And awe stilled now the throbbing at their hearts,
When suddenly one death-pale reveller starts
Up from the board and in shrill accent cries,
"Curst is this roof-tree, curst this meat and wine,
Fly, comrades; fly with me the wrath Divine!"

In haste, in horror, and great tumult, fled
The affrighted guests; then on the vacant room
No maddening voice thenceforth disquieted,
Fell the stern presence of a ghastly gloom.
A place 'twas deemed of hopeless, baleful doom;
Barred from all mortal view in darkness dread,
Only the spectral forms of woe and sin
Thro' the long years cold harborage found therein.

The Vengeance of the Goddess Diana.

[Sixteen years ago, in a volume of comparatively youthful verses, the following poem appeared under the title of "*Avolio ; A Legend of the Island of Cos.*" The original narrative has now been carefully rewritten and amended, and upwards of a hundred and fifty lines of entirely new matter have been added thereto. So far as we know, the only poet who has celebrated this significant and beautiful tradition, is William Morris, in the first section of whose "Earthly Paradise" there is a story (called "*The Lady of the Land*") founded upon some of its more obvious and popular incidents. Since Morris's wonderful tales were not published until 1868, we can, at least, assert the humble claim of precedence in the poetical treatment of *this* legend.]

What time the Norman ruled in Sicily,
At that mild season when the vernal sea,
O'erflitted by the zephyr's frolic wing,
Dances and dimples in the smile of Spring,
A goodly ship set sail upon her way
From Ceos unto Smyrna ; through the play
Of wave and sunbeam touched with fragrant calm,
She passed by beauteous island shores of palm,
Until so sweet the tender wooing breeze,
So fraught the hours with balms of slumbrous ease,
That those who manned her, in the genial air
And dalliance of the time, forgot the care
Due to her courses ; in the bland sunshine
They lay enchanted, dreaming dreams divine,

While idly drifting on the Halcyon water,
The bark obeyed whatever currents caught her.

Borne onward thus for many a cloudless day,
They reach at length a wide and wooded bay—
The haunt of birds whose purpling wings in flight
Make even the blushful morning seem more bright,
Flushed as with darting rainbows; through the tide,
By overripe pomegranate juices dyed,
And laving boughs of the wild fig and grape,
Great shoals of dazzling fishes madly ape
The play of silver lightnings in the deep
Translucent pools; the crew awoke from sleep,
Or rather that strange trance that on them pressed
Gently as sleep; yet still they loved to rest,
Fanned by voluptuous gales, by Morphean languors
　　blessed.
The shore sloped upward into foliaged hills,
Cleft by the channels of rock-fretted rills,
That flashed their wavelets, touched by iris lights,
O'er many a tiny cataract down the heights.

Green vales there were between, and pleasant lawns
Thick set with bloom, like sheen of tropic dawns,
Brightening the Orient; further still the glades

Of whisperous forests, flecked with golden shades,
Stretched glimmering southward; on the wood's far
    rim,
Faintly discerned thro' veiling vapors, dim
As mists of Indian Summer, the broad view
Was clasped by mountains flickering in the blue
And hazy distance; over all there hung
The morn's eternal beauty, calm and young.
Amid the throng, each with a marvelling face
Turned on that island Eden and its grace,
Was one—AVOLIO—a brave youth of Florence,
Self-exiled from his country, in abhorrence
Of the base, blood-stained tyrants dominant there.

A gentleman he was, of gracious air,
And liberal as the summer, skilled in lore
Of arms, and chivalry, and many more
Deep sciences which others' left unlearned.
He loved adventure; how his spirit burned
Within him, when, as now, a chance arose
To search untraveled forests, and strange foes
Vanquish by puissance of knightly blows,
Or rescue maidens from malignant spells,
Enforced by hordes of wizard sentinels.
So in the ardor of his martial glee,

He clapped his hands and shouted suddenly:
"Ho! sirs, a challenge! let us pierce these woods
Down to the core; explore their solitudes,
And make the flowery empire all our own;
Who knows but we may conquer us a throne?
At least, bold feats await us, grand emprize
To win us favor in our ladies' eyes;
By Heaven! he is a coward who delays."

So saying, all his countenance ablaze
With passionate zeal, the youth sprang lightly up,
And with right lusty motion, filled a cup—
They brought him straightway—to the glistening
    brim
With Cyprus wine: "Now glory unto him,
The ardent knight, no mortal danger daunts,
Whose constant soul a fiery impulse haunts,
Which spurs him onward, onward, to the end;
Pledge we the brave! and may St. Ermo send
Success to crown our valiantest!"
               —this said,
AVOLIO shoreward leaped, and with him led
The whole ship's company.

               —A motley band
Were they who mustered round him on the strand,

Mixed knights and traders; the first fired for toil
Which promised glory; the last keen for spoil!
Thro' breezy paths and beds of blossoming thyme
Kept fresh by secret springs, the showery chime
Of whose clear falling waters in the dells
Played like an airy peal of elfin bells—
With eager minds, but aimless, idle feet,
(The scene about them was so lone and sweet
It spelled their steps,) 'mid labyrinths of flowers,
By mossy streams and in deep shadowed bowers,
They strayed from charm to charm thro' lengths of
    languid hours.
In thickets of wild fern and rustling broom,
The humble bee buzzed past them with a boom
Of insect thunder; and in glens afar
The golden firefly—a small animate star—
Shone from the twilight of the darkling leaves.
High noon it was, but dusk like mellow eve's
Reigned in the wood's deep places, whence it seemed
That flashing locks and quick arch glances gleamed
From eyes scarce human. Thus the fancy deemed
Of those most given to marvels; the rest laughed
A merry, jeering laugh; and many a shaft
Launched from the Norman cross bow, pierced the
    nooks,

Or cleft the shallow channels of the brooks,
Whence, as the credulous swore, an Oread shy,
Or a glad Nymph, had peeped out cunningly.

Thus wandering, they reached a sombre mound
Rising abruptly from the level ground,
And planted thick with dim funereal trees,
Whose foliage waved and murmured, tho' the breeze
Had sunk to midnight quiet, and the sky
Just o'er the place seemed locked in apathy,
Like a fair face wan with the sudden stroke
Of death, or heart-break. Not a word they spoke,
But paused with wide, bewildered, gleaming eyes,
Standing at gaze; what spectral terrors rise
And coil about their hearts with serpent fold,
And oh ! what loathly scene is this they hold,
Grasped with unwinking vision, as they creep,
Urged by their very horror, up the steep,
And the whole preternatural landscape dawns
Freezingly on them ; a broad stretch of lawns,
Sown with rank poisonous grasses, where the dew
Of hovering exhalations flickered blue
And wavering on the dead-still atmosphere-
Dead-still it was, and yet the grasses sere
Stirred as with horrid life amidst the sickening
  glare.

The affrighted crew, all save AVOLIO, fled
In wild disorder from this place of dread;
In him, albeit his terror whispered "fly!"
The spell of some uncouth necessity
Baffled retreat, and ruthless, scourged him on;
Meanwhile, the sun thro' darkening vapors shone,
Nigh to his setting, and a sudden blast—
Sudden and chill—woke shrilly up, and passed
With ghostly din and tumult; airy sounds
Of sylvan horns, and sweep of circling hounds
Nearing the quarry.   Now the wizard chase
Swept faintly, faintly up the fields of space,
And now with backward rushing whirl roared by
Louder and fiercer, till a maddening cry—
A bitter shriek of human agony—
Leaped up, and died amid the stifling yell
Of brutes athirst for blood; a crowning swell
Of savage triumph followed, mixed with wails
Sad as the dying songs of nightingales,
Murmuring the name ACTÆON!

                                    Even as one,
A wrapt sleep-walker, through the shadows dun
Of half oblivious sense, with soulless gaze,
Goes idly journeying through uncertain ways,
Thus did AVOLIO, sore perplexed in mind

(Excess of mystery made his spirit blind),
Grope through the gloom. Anon he reached a fount
Whose watery columns had long ceased to mount
Above its prostrate Tritons. Near at hand,
Dammed up in part by heaps of tawny sand,
All dull and lustreless, a streamlet wound
Of trickling banks, with dark, dank foliage crowned,
That gloomed 'twixt sullen tides and lowering sky;
The melancholy waters seemed to sigh
In wailful murmurs of articulate woe,
Till at the last arose this strange dirge from below:

SONG OF THE IMPRISONED NAIAD.

" Woe! woe is me! the centuries pass away,
   The mortal seasons run their ceaseless rounds,
  While here I wither for the sunbright day,
   Its genial sights and sounds.
              Woe! woe is me!

"One summer night, in ages long agone,
  I saw my Oread lover leave the brake;
I heard him plaining on the peaceful lawn
  A plaint ' for my sweet sake.'
              Woe! woe is me!

"My heart upsprang to answer that fond lay,
    But suddenly the star girt planets paled,
And high into the welkin's glimmering gray
    Majestic DIAN sailed !

                    Woe ! woe is me !

" She swept aloft, bold almost as the sun,
    And wrathful red as fiery-crested Mars ;
Ah ! then I knew some fearful deed was done
    On earth, or in the stars.·

                    Woe ! woe is me !

" With ghastly face upraised, and shuddering throat,
    I watched the omen with a prescient pain ;
When, lightning-barbed, a beamy arrow smote,
    Or *seemed* to smite, my brain.

                    Woe ! woe is me !

" Oblivion clasped me, till I woke forlorn,
    Fettered and sorrowing on this lonely bed,
Shut from the mirthful kisses of the morn—
    Earth's glories overhead.

                    Woe ! woe is me !

" The south wind stirs the sedges into song,
    The blossoming myrtles scent the enamored air ;

But still, sore moaning for another's wrong,
  I pine in sadness here.
                    Woe! woe is me!

" Alas! alas! the weary centuries flee,
  The waning seasons perish, dark or bright;
My grief alone, like some charmed poison-tree,
  Knows not an autumn blight.
                    Woe! woe is me !"

The mournful sounds swooned off, but Echo rose,
And bore them up divinely to a close
Of rare mysterious sweetness; nevermore
Shall mortal winds to listening wood and shore
Waft such   heart-melting   music.   "Where, oh!
    where,"
AVOLIO murmured—" to what haunted sphere—
Has Fate at length my errant footsteps brought ?"

Launched on a baffling sea of mystic thought,
His reason in a whirling chaos, lost
Compass and chart and headway, vaguely tossed
'Mid shifting shapes of wingèd phantasies.

Just then, uplifting his bewildered eyes,
He saw, half hid in shade, on either hand,

Twin pillars of a massive gateway grand
With gold and carvings; close behind it stood
A sombre mansion in a beech tree wood.

Long wreaths of ghostly ivy on its walls
Quivered like goblin tapestry, or palls,
Tattered and rusty, mildewed in the chill
Of dreadful vaults; across each window sill
Curtains of weird device and fiery hue
Hung moveless—only when the sun glanced through
The gathering gloom the hieroglyphs took form
And life and action, and the whole grew warm
With meanings baffling to AVOLIO's sense;
He stood expectant, trembling, with intense
Dread in his eyes, and yet a struggling faith,
Vital at heart.   A sudden passing breath—
Was it the wind?—thrilled by his tingling ear,
Waving the curtains inward, and his fear
Uprose victorious, for a serpent shape—
Tall, supple, writhing, with malignant gape,
Which showed its cruel fangs—hissed in the gleam
Its own fell eyeballs kindled!   Oh! supreme
The horror of that vision!   As he gazed,
Irresolute, all wordless, and amazed,
The monster disappeared—a moment sped!

The next it fawned before him on a bed
Of scarlet poppies. " Speak !" AVOLIO said ;
" What art thou ? Speak ! I charge thee in God's
  name !"

A death cold shudder seized the serpent's frame,
Its huge throat writhed, whence bubbling with a
  throe
Of hideous import, a voice thin and low
Broke like a muddied rill : " Bethink thee well,
" This isle is Cos, of which old legends tell
" Such marvels. Hast thou never heard of me,
" The island's fated queen ?" " Yea, verily,"
AVOLIO cried, " thou art that thing of dread——"
Sharply the serpent raised its glittering head
And front tempestuous : " Hold ! no tongue save
  mine
" Must of these miseries tell thee ! Then incline
" Thine ear to the dark story of my grief,
" And with thine ear yield, yield me thy belief.
" Foul as I am, there *was* a time, O youth,
" When these fierce eyes were founts of love and
  truth ;
" There *was* a time when woman's blooming grace
" Glowed through the flush of roses in my face ;

" When—but I sinned a deep and damning sin,
" The fruit of lustful pride nurtured within
" By weird, forbidden knowledge—I defied
" The night's immaculate goddess, purest eyed,
" And holiest of immortals; I denied
" The eternal Power that looks so cold and calm ;
" Therefore, O stranger, am I what I am,
" A monster meet for Tartarus, a thing
" Whereon men gaze with awe and shuddering,
" And stress of inward terror; through all time,
" Down to the last age, my abhorrèd crime
" Must hold me prisoner in this vile abode,
" *Unless some man, large-hearted as a God,*
" *Bolder than Ajax, mercifully deign*
" *To kiss me on the mouth !"*

       She towered amain,
With sparkling crest, and universal thrill
Of frenzied eagerness, that seemed to fill
Her cavernous eyes with jets of lurid fire,
Pulsed from the burning core of unappeased desire.

Back stepped AVOLIO with a loathing fear,
Sick to the inmost soul; then did he hear
The awful creature vent a tortured groan,
Her frantic neck and dragon's forehead thrown

Madly to earth, whereon awhile she lay,
Her glances veiled, her dark crest turned away.

As thus she grovelled, quivering on the ground,
Stole through the brooding silence a faint sound
As 'twere of hopeless grief—it seemed to be
A human voice weeping how piteously!
Yet its deep passion striving to subdue.
Just then the serpent writhed her folds anew,
And while from earth her horrent crest she rears,
The loathly creature's face is bathed in tears!

"Lady!" the knight said, "if in sooth thou art
"A maid and human, wherefore thus depart
"From truth's plain path to blind me? well I know
"This DIAN, famed and worshipped long ago
"By heathen folk, was as the idle fume
"Formed into shifting shapes of vaporous bloom
"O'er her vain altars.   Ah!" (he shuddered now,
Growing death pale from tremulous chin to brow)
"*Ah, God! I cannot kiss thee!*   Ne'ertheless,
"Fain am I in the true God's name to bless,
"And even to mark thee with HIS sacred cross!"

As one weighed down by anguish and the loss
Of one last hope, in faltering tones and sad

The serpent spake : " Deem'st thou that DIAN had
" No life but that wherewith her votaries vain
" Invested a vague image of the brain ?
" Nay, she both *was* and *was not*, as on earth,
" Even to this day, full many a thing from birth
" To death lapses alike through bane and bliss;
" Full many a thing, which is not and yet is,
" Save to man's purblind vision ;—in the end
" Some clearer spirits may rise to comprehend
" This strange enigma ! but meanwhile, meanwhile
" The sure heavens change not, star and sunbeam
        smile
" Fair as of yore; eternal nature keeps
" Her strength and beauty, though the mortal
        weeps
" In desolation !   Oh ! wert *thou* but true
" And brave enow this thing I ask to do,
" Then human, happy, beauteous would I be,
" Ye merciful Gods ! once more !"

                    Then suddenly
She writhed her vast neck round, her glittering
        crest
Cast backward o'er the fierce, tumultuous breast,
Red as a stormy sunset—with a moan,

" Pass on, weak soul !" she said, " leave me alone ;"
Then, wildly, "Go ! I would not catch thine eye ;
" *Go, and be safe !* for swiftly, furiously,
" Surges a cruel thought through all my blood,
" And the brute instincts turn to hardihood
" Of vengeful impulse all my gentler frame ;
" Go ! for I would not harm thee ; yet a flame
" Of blasting torments have I power to raise
" Through all thy being, and mine eyes *could* gaze,
" Gloating on pain.   Is this not horrible ?"
And therewithal the wretched monster fell
To open weeping, with sad front, and bowed.

Something in such base cruelty avowed,
Blent with the softer will which disallowed
Its exercise, so on AVOLIO wrought,
That sore perplexed, revolving many a thought,
He lingered still, lost in a spiritual mist ;
But when the mouth that waited to be kissed,
Fringed with a yellow foam, malignly rose
Before him, his first fear its terrible throes
Renewed.   " And how, O baleful shape !" said he—
Striving to speak in passionless tones, and free—
" How can I tell, what certain gage have I,
" That this strange kiss thine awful destiny

" Hath not ordained—the least elaborate plan

" Whereby to snare and slay me?" "O man!
    man!"

The serpent answered, with a loftier mien—

A voice grown clear, majestic and serene—

" Shall MATTER always triumph? the base mould

" Mask the immortal essence, uncontrolled

" Save by your grovelling fancies mean and cold?

" O green and happy woods, breathing like sleep!

" O quiet habitants of places deep

" In leafy shades, that draw your peaceful breaths,

" Passing fair lives to rest in tranquil deaths!

" O earth! O sea! O heavens! forever dumb ·

" To man, while ages go and ages come

" Mysterious, have the dark Fates willed it so

" That nevermore the sons of men shall know

" The secret of your silence? the wide scope

" Granted your basking pleasures, and sweet hope,

" Revived in vernal warmth and springtide rains,

" Your long, long pleasures, and your fleeting
    pains?

" And must the lack of what is brave and true,

" From other souls, callous or blind thereto,

" From what themselves beauteous and truthful are,

" Differ for aye as glow-worms from a star?

" Is such our life's decretal ? Shall the faith
" Which even, perchance, the clearest spirit hath
" In good within us, always prove less bold
" Than keen suspicions, nursed by craven doubt,
" Of treacherous ills, and evil from without ?"
Then, after pause, with passion : " O etern
" And bland Benignities, that breathe and burn
" Throughout creation, are we but the motes
" In some vague dream that idly sways and floats
" To nothingness ? or are your glories pent
" Within ourselves, to rise omnipotent
" In bloom, and music, when we bend above,
" And wake them by the kisses of our love ?
" I yearn to be made beautiful.   Alas !
" Beauty itself looks on, prepared to pass,
" In hardened disbelief ! *one* action kind
" Would free and save me—why art thou so blind,
" AVOLIO ?"
        While she spoke, a timorous hare,
Scared by a threatening falcon from its lair,
Rushed to the serpent's side.   With fondling tongue
She soothed it as a mother soothes her young.

AVOLIO mused : " Can innocent things like this
" Take refuge by her ? then, perchance, some good,

" Some tenderness, if rightly understood,
" Lurks in her nature.   *I will do the deed!*
" *Christ and the Virgin save me at my need.*"

He signed the monster nearer, closed his eyes,
And with some natural shuddering, some deep sighs,
Gave up his pallid lips to the foul kiss !
What followed then ? a traitorous serpent hiss,
Sharper for triumph ?   Ah ! not so—he felt
A warm, rich, yearning mouth approach and melt
In languid, loving sweetness on his own,
And two fond arms caressingly were thrown
About his neck, and on his bosom pressed
Twin lilies of a snow white virgin breast.

He raised his eyes, released from brief despair ;
They rested on a maiden tall and fair—
Fair as the tropic morn, when morn is new—
And her sweet glances smote him through and
       through
With such keen thrilling rapture that he swore
His willing heart should evermore adore
Her loveliness, and woo her till he died.

" I am thine own," she whispered, " thy true bride,
" If thou wilt take me !"

Hand in hand they strayed
Adown the shadows through the woodland glade,
Whence every evil Influence shrank afraid,
And round them poured the golden eventide.
Swiftly the tidings of this strange event
Abroad on all the garrulous winds were sent,
Rousing an eager world to wonderment!

Now, 'mid the knightly companies that came
To visit Cos, was that brave chief, by fame
Exalted for bold deeds and faith divine,
So nobly shown erewhile in Palestine—
Tancred, Salerno's Prince—he came in state,
With fourscore gorgeous barges, small and great,
With pomp and music, like an ocean Fate;
His blazoned prows along the glimmering sea
Spread like an Eastern sunrise gloriously.

Him and his followers did AVOLIO feast
Right royally, but when the mirth increased,
And joyous-wingéd jests began to pass
Above the sparkling cups of Hippocras,
Tancred arose, and in his courtly phrase
Invoked delight and length of prosperous days
To crown that magic union; one vague doubt

The Prince did move, and this he dared speak out,
But with serene and tempered courtesy :
" It could not be that their sweet hostess still
" Worshipped Diana and her heathen will ?"

" Ah sir ! not so !" AVOLIO flushing cried,
" But Christ the Lord !"
              No single word replied
The beauteous lady, but with gentle pride
And a quick motion to AVOLIO's side
She drew more closely by a little space,
Gazing with modest passion in his face,
As one who yearned to whisper tenderly :
" *O, brave, kind heart ! I worship only thee !*"

The Voice in the Pines.

The morn is softly beautiful and still,
  Its light fair clouds in pencilled gold and gray
Pause motionless above the pine-grown hill,
Where the pines, tranced as by a wizard's will,
  Uprise, as mute and motionless as they!

Yea! mute and moveless; not one flickering spray
  Flashed into sunlight, nor a gaunt bough stirred;
Yet, if wooed hence beneath those pines to stray,
We catch a faint, thin murmur far away,
  A bodiless voice, by grosser ears unheard.

What voice is this? what low and solemn tone,
  Which, though all wings of all the winds seem
      furled,
Nor even the zephyr's fairy flute is blown,
Makes thus forever its mysterious moan
  From out the whispering pine-tops' shadowy world?

Ah! can it be the antique tales are true?
  Doth some lone Dryad haunt the breezeless air, .
Fronting yon bright immitigable blue,

And wildly breathing all her wild soul through
    That strange, unearthly music of despair?

Or can it be that ages since, storm-tossed,
    And driven far inland from the roaring lea,
Some baffled ocean-spirit, worn and lost,
Here, through dry summer's dearth and winter's
      frost,
    Yearns for the sharp, sweet kisses of the sea?

Whate'er the spell, I hearken and am dumb,
    Dream-touched, and musing in the tranquil morn;
All woodland sounds—the pheasant's gusty drum,
The mockbird's fugue, the droning insect's hum—
    Scarce heard for that strange, sorrowful voice for-
      lorn!

Beneath the drowséd sense, from deep to deep
    Of spiritual life its mournful minor flows,
Streamlike, with pensive tide, whose currents keep
Low murmuring 'twixt the bounds of grief and sleep,
    Yet locked for aye from sleep's divine repose.

The Solitary Lake.

From garish light and life apart,
Shrined in the woodland's secret heart,
With delicate mists of morning furled
Fantastic o'er its shadowy world,
The lake, a vaporous vision, gleams
So vaguely bright, my fancy deems
'Tis but an airy lake of dreams.

Dreamlike, in curves of palest gold,
The wavering mist-wreaths manifold
Part in long rifts, through which I view
Gray islets throned in tides as blue
As if a piece of heaven withdrawn—
Whence hints of sunrise touch the dawn—
Had brought to earth its sapphire glow,
And smiled, a second heaven, below.

Dreamlike, in fitful, murmurous sighs,
I hear the distant west wind rise,
And, down the hollows wandering, break
In gurgling ripples on the lake,

Round which the vapors, still outspread,
Mount wanly widening overhead,
Till flushed by morning's primrose-red.

Dreamlike, each slow, soft-pulsing surge
Hath lapped the calm lake's emerald verge,
Sending, where'er its tremors pass
Low whisperings through the dew-wet grass;
Faint thrills of fairy sound that creep
To fall in neighboring nooks asleep,
Or melt in rich, low warblings made
By some winged Ariel of the glade.

With brightening morn the mockbird's
Grows stronger, mellower; far away
'Mid dusky reeds, which even the noon
Lights not, the lonely-hearted loon
Makes answer, her shrill music shorn
Of half its sadness; day, full-born,
Doth rout all sounds and sights forlorn.

Ah! still a something strange and rare
O'errules this tranquil earth and air,
Casting o'er both a glamour known
To *their* enchanted realm alone;

Whence shines, as 'twere a spirit's face,
The sweet, coy Genius of the place—
Yon Lake, beheld as if in trance—
The beauty of whose shy romance
I feel—whatever shores and skies
May charm henceforth my wondering eyes,
Shall rest, undimmed by taint or stain,
'Mid lonely byways of the brain,
There, with its haunting grace, to seem
Set in the landscape of a dream.

Visit of the Wrens.

Flying from out the gusty west,
To seek the place where last year's nest,
Ragged, and torn by many a rout
Of winter winds, still rocks about
The branches of the gnarled old tree
Which sweep my cottage library—
Here on the genial southern side,
In a late gleam of sunset's pride,
Came back my tiny, springtide friends,
The self-same pair of chattering wrens
That with arch eyes and restless bill
Used to frequent yon window sill,
Winged sprites, in April's showery glow.

'Tis now twelve weary months ago
Since first I saw them; here again
They drop outside the glittering pane,
Each bearing a dried twig or leaf,
To build with labor hard, yet brief,
This season's nest, where, blue and round,
Their fairy eggs will soon be found.

But sky and breeze and blithesome sun,
Until that little home is done,
Shall—wondering, maybe—hear and see
Such chatter, bustle, industry,
As well may stir to emulous strife
Slow currents of a languid life,
Whether in bird or man they run !

But when, in sooth, the nest complete
Swings gently in its green retreat,
And soft the mother birdling's breast
Doth in the cozy circlet rest,
How, back from jovial journeying,
Merry of heart, though worn of wing,
Her brown mate, proudly perched above
The limb that holds his brooding love,
His head upturned, his aspect sly,
Regards her with a cunning eye,
As one who saith, " How well you bear
The dullness of these duties, dear ;
To dwell so long on nest or tree
Would be, I know, slow death to me ;
But, then, you women folk were made
For patient waiting, in—the shade !"

So tame one little guest becomes—
'Tis the male bird—my scattered crumbs

He takes from window sill and lawn
Each morning in the early dawn;
And yesterday he dared to stand
Serenely on my outstretched hand,
While his wee wife, with puzzled glance,
Looked from her breezy seat askance!

My pretty pensioners! ye have flown
Twice from your winter nook unknown,
To build your humble homestead here,
In the first flush of springtide cheer;
But ah! I wonder if again,
Flitting outside the window pane,
When next the shrewd March winds shall blow,
Or in mild April's showers glow,
New come from out the shimmering West,
You'll seek the place of this year's nest,
Ragged and torn by then, no doubt,
And swinging in worn shreds about
The branches of the ancient tree.

Nay, who may tell? Yet, verily,
Methinks when, spring and summer passed,
Adown the long, low autumn blast,
In some dim gloaming, chill and drear,

You, with your fledglings, disappear,
That ne'er by porch or tree or pane
Mine eyes shall greet your forms again !

What then ?　At least the good ye brought,
The delicate charms for eye and thought
Survives; though death should be your doom
Before another spring flower's bloom,
Or fairer clime should tempt your wings
To bide 'mid fragrant blossomings
On some far Southland's golden lea,
Still may fresh spring morns light for me
Your tiny nest, their breezes bear
Your chirping, household joyance near,
And all your quirks and tricksome ways
Bring back through many smiling days
Or future Aprils; not the less
Your simple drama shall impress
Fancy and heart, thus acted o'er
Toward each small issue, as of yore,
With sun and wind and skies of blue
To witness, wondering, all you do,
Because your happy toil and mirth
May be of fine, ideal birth ;
Because each quick, impulsive note

May thrill a visionary throat,
Each flash of glancing wing and eye
Be gleams of vivid fantasy ;
Since whatsoe'er of form and tone
A past reality hath known,
Most charming unto soul and sense,
But wins that subtle effluence,
That spiritual air which softly clings
About all sweet and vanished things,
Causing a bygone joy to be
Vital as actuality,
Yet with each earthlier tint or trace
Lost in a pure, ethereal grace !

Aspects of the Pines.

Tall, sombre, grim, against the morning sky
   They rise, scarce touched by melancholy airs,
Which stir the fadeless foliage dreamfully,
   As if from realms of mystical despairs.

Tall, sombre, grim, they stand with dusky gleams
   Brightening to gold within the woodland's core,
Beneath the gracious noontide's tranquil beams—
   But the weird winds of morning sigh no more.

A stillness, strange, divine, ineffable,
   Broods round and o'er them in the wind's surcease.
And on each tinted copse and shimmering dell
   Rests the mute rapture of deep hearted peace.

Last, sunset comes—the solemn joy and might
   Borne from the West when cloudless day declines—
Low, flutelike breezes sweep the waves of light,
   And lifting dark green tresses of the pines,

Till every lock is luminous—gently float,
   Fraught with hale odors up the heavens afar
To faint when Twilight on her virginal throat
   Wears for a gem the tremulous vesper star.

Forest Pictures.

MORNING.

O gracious breath of sunrise! divine air!
 That brood'st serenely o'er the purpling hills;
O blissful valleys! nestling, cool and fair,
 In the fond arms of yonder murmurous rills,
Breathing their grateful measures to the sun;
O dew-besprinkled paths, that circling run
Through sylvan shades and solemn silences,
Once more ye bring my fevered spirit peace!

The fitful breezes, fraught with forest balm,
 Faint, in rare wafts of perfume, on my brow;
The woven lights and shadows, rife with calm,
 Creep slantwise 'twixt the foliage, bough on bough
Uplifted heavenward, like a verdant cloud
Whose rain is music, soft as love, or loud
With jubilant hope—for there, entranced, apart,
The mock-bird sings, close, close to Nature's heart.

Shy forms about the greenery, out and in,
 Flit 'neath the broadening glories of the morn;
The squirrel—that quaint sylvan harlequin—
 Mounts the tall trunks; while swift as lightning, born

Of summer mists, from tangled vine and tree
Dart the dove's pinions, pulsing vividly
Down the dense glades, till glimmering far and gray
The dusky vision softly melts away!

In transient, pleased bewilderment, I mark
The last dim shimmer of those lessening wings,
When from lone copse and shadowy covert, hark!
What mellow tongue through all the woodland
rings!
The deer-hound's voice, sweet as the golden bell's,
Prolonged by flying echoes round the dells,
And up the loftiest summits wildly borne,
Blent with the blast of some keen huntsman's horn.

And now the checkered vale is left behind;
I climb the slope, and reach the hilltop bright;
Here, in bold freedom, swells a sovereign wind,
Whose gusty prowess sweeps the pine clad height;
While the pines—dreamy Titans roused from sleep—
Answer with mighty voices, deep on deep
Of wakened foliage surging like a sea;
And o'er them smiles Heaven's calm infinity!

Golden Dell.

Beyond our moss-grown pathway lies
A dell so fair, to genial eyes
It dawns an ever-fresh surprise!

To touch its charms with gentler grace,
The softened heavens a loving face
Bend o'er that sweet, secluded place.

There first, despite the March wind's cold,
Above the pale-hued emerald mould
The earliest spring-tide buds unfold;

There first the ardent mock-bird, long
Winter's dumb thrall, from winter's wrong
Breaks into gleeful floods of song;

Till, from coy thrush to garrulous wren,
The humbler bards of copse and glen
Outpour their vernal notes again;

While such harmonious rapture rings,
With stir and flash of eager wings
Glimpsed fleetly, where the jasmine clings

To bosk and briar, we blithely say,
" Farewell! bleak nights and mornings gray,
Earth opes her festal court to-day !"

There, first, from out some balmy nest,
By half-grown woodbine flowers caressed,
Steal zephyrs of the mild southwest;

O'er purpling rows of wild-wood peas,*
So blandly borne, the droning bees
Still suck their honeyed cores at ease;

Or, trembling through you verdurous mass,
Dew-starred, and dimpling as they pass
The wavelets of the billowy grass!

But, fairest of fair things that dwell
'Mid sylvan nurslings of the dell,
Is that clear stream whose murmurs swell

To music's airiest issues wrought,
As if a Naiad's tongue were fraught
With secrets of its whispered thought.

Yes, fairest of fair things, it flows
'Twixt banks of violet and of rose,
Touched always by a quaint repose.

---

* In the Southern woods, often among sterile tracts of pine barren, a
species of *wild pea* is found, or a plant which in all externals resembles the
pea plant.

How golden bright its currents glide!
While goldenly from side to side
Bird-shadows flit athwart the tide.

So Golden Dell we name the place,
And aye may Heaven's serenest face
Dream o'er it with a smile of grace;

For next the moss-growth path it lies,
So pure, so fresh, to genial eyes
It glows with hints of Paradise!

Cloud=Pictures.

Here, in these mellow grasses, the whole morn,
I love to rest; yonder, the ripening corn
Rustles its greenery: and his blithesome horn

Windeth the frolic breeze o'er field and dell,
Now pealing a bold stave with lusty swell,
Now falling to low breaths ineffable

Of whispered joyance. At calm length I lie,
Fronting the broad blue spaces of the sky,
Covered with cloud-groups, softly journeying by:

An hundred shapes, fantastic, beauteous, strange,
Is theirs, as o'er yon airy waves they range
At the wind's will, from marvellous change to
    change;

Castles, with guarded roof, and turret tall,
Great sloping archway, and majestic wall,
Sapped by the breezes to their noiseless fall!

Pagodas vague! above whose towers outstream
Banners that wave with motions of a dream—
Rising, or drooping in the noontide gleam;

Gray lines of Orient pilgrims: a gaunt band
On famished camels, o'er the desert sand
Plodding towards their Prophet's Holy Land;

'Mid-ocean,—and a shoal of whales at play,
Lifting their monstrous frontlets to the day,
Thro' rainbow arches of sun-smitten spray;

Followed by splintered icebergs, vast and lone,
Set in swift currents of some arctic zone,
Like fragments of a Titan's world o'erthrown;

Next, measureless breadths of barren, treeless moor,
Whose vaporous verge fades down a glimmering
      shore,
Round which the foam-capped billows toss and roar!

Calms of bright water—like a fairy's wiles,
Wooing, with ripply cadence and soft smiles,
The golden shore-slopes of Hesperian Isles;

Their inland plains rife with a rare increase
Of plumèd grain! and many a snowy fleece
Shining athwart the dew-lit hills of peace;

Wrecks of gigantic cities—to the tune
Of some wise air-God built!—o'er which the Noon
Seems shuddering; caverns, such as the wan Moon

Shows in her desolate bosom; then, a crowd
Of awed and reverent faces, palely bowed
O'er a dead queen, laid in her ashy shroud—

A queen of eld—her pallid brow impearled
By gems barbaric!—her strange beauty furled
In mystic cerements of the antique world.

Weird pictures, fancy-gendered!—one by one,
'Twixt blended beams and shadows, gold and dun,
These transient visions vanish in the sun.

Midsummer in the South.

I love Queen August's stately sway,
And all her fragrant south winds say,
With vague, mysterious meanings fraught,
Of unimaginable thought;
Those winds, 'mid change of gloom and gleam,
Seem wandering thro' a golden dream—
The rare midsummer dream that lies
In humid depths of Nature's eyes,
Weighing her languid forehead down
Beneath a fair but fiery crown:
Its witchery broods o'er earth and skies—
Fills with divine amenities
The bland, blue spaces of the air,
And smiles with looks of drowsy cheer
'Mid hollows of the brown-hued hills;
And oft, in tongues of tinkling rills,
A softer, homelier utterance finds
Than that which haunts the lingering winds!

I love midsummer's azure deep,
Whereon the huge white clouds, asleep,

Scarce move through lengths of trancéd hours;
Some, raised in forms of giant towers—
Dumb Babels, with ethereal stairs
Scaling the vast height—unawares
What mocking spirit, æther·born,
Hath built those transient spires in scorn,
And reared towards the topmost sky
Their unsubstantial fantasy!
Some stretched in tenuous arcs of light
Athwart the airy infinite,
Far glittering up yon fervid dome,
And lapped by Cloudland's misty foam,
Whose wreaths of fine sun-smitten spray
Melt in a burning haze away:
Some throned in heaven's serenest smiles,
Pure-hued, and calm as fairy isles,
Girt by the tides of soundless seas—
The heavens' benign Hesperides.

I love midsummer uplands, free
To the bold raids of breeze and bee,
Where, nested warm in yellowing grass,
I hear the swift-winged partridge pass,
With whirr and boom of gusty flight,
Across the broad heath's treeless height:

Or, just where, elbow-poised, I lift
Above the wild flower's careless drift
My half-closed eyes, I see and hear
The blithe field-sparrow twittering clear
Quick ditties to his tiny love;
While, from afar, the timid dove,
With faint, voluptuous murmur, wakes
The silence of the pastoral brakes.

I love midsummer sunsets, rolled
Down the rich west in waves of gold,
With blazing crests of billowy fire.
But when those crimson floods retire,
In noiseless ebb, slow-surging, grand,
By pensive twilight's flickering strand,
In gentler mood I love to mark
The slow gradations of the dark;
Till, lo! from Orient's mists withdrawn,
Hail! to the Moon's resplendent dawn;
On dusky vale and haunted plain
Her effluence falls like balmy rain;
Gaunt gulfs of shadow own her might;
She bathes the rescued world in light,
So that, albeit my Summer's Day
Erewhile did breathe its life away,

Methinks, whate'er its hours had won
Of beauty, born from shade and sun,
Hath not perchance so wholly died,
But o'er the moonlight's silvery tide
Comes back, sublimed and purified!

In the Pine Barrens.

SUNSET.

Hark! to the mournful wind; its burden drear
  Borne over leagues of desert wild and dun,
Sinks to a weary cadence of despair,
  Beyond the closing gateways of the Sun.

Yon clouds are big with flame, and not with rain,
  Massed on the marvellous heaven in splendid
    pyres,
Whereon ethereal genii, half in pain
  And half in triumph, light their fervid fires;

Kindled in funeral majesty to rise
  Above the perished Day, whose latest breath
Exhaled, a roseate effluence to the skies,
  Still lingers o'er the pageantry of death.

   *   *   *   *   *   *   *   *

One stalwart hill his stern defiant crest
  Boldly against the horizon line uprears,
His blasted Pines, smit by the fiery West,
  Uptowering rank on rank, like Titan spears;

Fantastic, bodeful, o'er the rock-strewn ground
   Casting grim shades beyond the hill slope riven,
Which mock the loftier shafts, keen, lustre-crowned
   And raised as if to storm the courts of Heaven!

As sinks the wind, so wane those wondrous lights;
   Slowly they wane from hill and sky and cloud,
While round the woodland waste and glimmering
     heights
The mist of gloaming trails its silvery shroud!

Through which, uncertain, vague as shifting ghosts,
   The forms of all things touched by mystery seem,
I walk, methinks, on pale Plutonian coasts,
   And grope 'mid spectral shadows of a dream.

The Woodland Phases.

Yon woodland, like a human mind,
  Hath many a phase of dark and bright;
Now dim with shadows, wandering blind,
  Now radiant with fair shapes of light.

They softly come, they softly go,
  Capricious as the vagrant wind—
Nature's vague thoughts in gloom or glow,
  That leave no airiest trace behind.

No trace, no trace! yet wherefore thus
  Do shade and beam our spirits stir?
Ah! Nature may be cold to us,
  But we are strangely moved by her.

The wild bird's strain, the breezy spray—
  Each hour with sure earth-changes rife—
Hint more than all the sages say,
  Or poets sing of death and life.

For, truths half drawn from Nature's breast,
  Through subtlest types of form and tone,

Outweigh what man, at most, hath guessed
    While heeding his own heart alone.

And midway, betwixt heaven and us,
    Stands Nature, in her fadeless grace,
Still pointing to our Father's house,
    His glory on her mystic face.

Sonnet.

Sunset, the god-like artist paints on air
Pictures of loveliness and terror blent:
Lo! yonder clouds, like mountains tempest-rent,
Through whose abysmal depths the lightning's glare
Darts from wild gulfs and caverns of despair:
O'er these a calm, majestic firmament,
Flushed with rich hues, with rainbow isles besprent,
Like homes of peace in oceans heavenly fair:

But *still*, beyond, one lone mysterious cloud,
Steeped in the solemn sunset's fiery mist,
Strange semblance takes of Him whose visage bowed,
Divinely sweet, o'er all things, dark or bright,
Yet draws the darkness ever toward His light—
The tender eyes and awful brow of Christ!

Sonnet.

In the deep hollow of this sheltered dell
I hear the rude winds chant their giant staves
Far, far beyond me, where in darkening waves
The airy seas of cloud-land sink or swell.

No faint breeze stirs the wild flower's soundless bell,
Here in the quiet vale, whose rivulet laves
Banks silent almost as those desert graves,
Whereof the worn Zaharan wanderers tell.

Oh! thus from out still depths of tranquil doom,
My soul beyond her views life's turmoil vast,
Hearkening the windy roar and rage of men,

Vain to *her* eyes as shades from cloud-land cast,
And to *her* ears like far-off winds that boom,
Heard, but scarce heard, in this Arcadian glen !

After the Tornado.

Last eve the earth was calm, the heavens were clear;
A peaceful glory crowned the waning west,
And yonder distant mountain's hoary crest
The semblance of a silvery robe did wear,
Shot through with moon-wrought tissues; far and
        near
Wood, rivulet, field—all Nature's face—expressed
The haunting presence of enchanted rest.
One twilight star shone like a blissful tear,
Unshed.   But now, what ravage in a night!
You mountain height fades in its cloud-girt pall;
The prostrate wood lies smirched with rain and mire;
Through the shorn fields the brook whirls, wild and
        white;
While o'er the turbulent waste, and woodland fall,
Glares the red sunrise, blurred with mists of fire!

By the Grave of Henry Timrod.

When last we parted—thy frail hand in mine—
Above us smiled September's passionless sky,
And touched by fragrant airs, the hill-side pine
Thrilled in the mellow sunshine tenderly;
So rich the robe on nature's slow decay,
We scarce could deem the Winter tide was near,
Or lurking death, masked in imperial grace;
Alas! that Autumn day
Drew not more close to Winter's empire drear
Than thou, my heart! to meet grief face to face!

I clasped thy tremulous hand, nor marked how
weak
Its answering grasp; and if thine eyes did swim
In unshed tears, and on thy fading cheek
Rested a nameless shadow, gaunt and dim,—
My soul was blind; fear had not touched her
sight
To awful vision; so, I bade thee go,
Careless, and tranquil as that treacherous morn;
Nor dreamed how soon the blight

Of long-implanted seeds of care would throw
　　Their nightshade flowers above the springing
　　　　corn.

Since then, full many a year hath risen and set,
　　With Spring-tide showers, and Autumn pomps
　　　　unfurled
O'er gorgeous woods, and mountain walls of jet—
　　While love and loss, alternate, ruled the world;
　　　　Till now once more we meet—my friend and I—
Once more, once more—and thus, alas! we meet—
　　Above, a rayless heaven; beneath, a grave;
　　　　Oh, Christ! and dost thou lie
Neglected here, in thy worn burial-sheet?
　　Friend! were there none to shield thee, none to
　　　　save?

Ask of the Winter winds—scarce colder they
　　Than that strange land—thy birth place and thy
　　　　tomb:
Ask of the sombre cloud-wracks trooping gray,
　　And grim as hooded ghosts at stroke of doom;
　　　　At least, the winds, though chill, with gentler
　　　　　　sweep
Seem circling round and o'er thy place of rest,

While the sad clouds, as clothed in tenderer
 guise,
  Do lowly bend, and weep
O'er the dead Poet, in whose living breast
  Dumb nature found a voice, how sweet and wise!

Once more we meet, once more—my friend and I—
  But ah! his hand is dust, his eyes are dark;
Thy merciless weight, thou dread mortality,
  From out his heart hath crushed the latest spark
   Of that warm life, benignly bright and strong;
Yet no; we have *not* met—my friend and I—
  Ashes to ashes in this earthly prison!
   Are these, O child of song,
Thy glorious self, heir of the stars and sky?
Thou art not here, not *here*, for thou hast risen!

Death gave thee wings, and lo! thou hast soared
 above
  All human utterance and all finite thought;
Pain may not hound thee through that realm of
 love,
  Nor grief, wherewith thy mortal days were
  fraught,
   Load thee again—nor vulture want, that fed

Even on thy heart's blood, wound thee; idle, then,
  Our bitter sorrowing; what though bleak and
    wild
  Rests thine uncrownèd head?
Known art thou now to angels and to men—
  Heaven's saint, and earth's brave singer un-
    defiled.

Even as I spake in broken under-breath
  The winds drooped lifeless; faintly struggling
    through
The heaven-bound pall, which seemed a pall of
    death,
  One cordial sunbeam cleft the opening blue;
    Swiftly it glanced, and settling, softly shone
O'er the grave's head; in that same instant came
  From the near copse a bird-song half divine;
    " Heart," said I, " Hush thy moan,
List the bird's singing, mark the heaven-born flame,
  God-given are these—an omen and a sign!"

In the bird's song an omen *his* must live!
  In the warm glittering of that golden beam,
A sign his soul's majestic hopes survive,
  Raised to fruition o'er life's weary dream.
    So now I leave him, low, yet restful here;

So now I leave him, high-exalted, far
　　Beyond all memory of earth's guilt or guile;
　　　Hark! 'tis his voice of cheer,
Dropping, methinks, from some mysterious star;
　　His face I see, and on his face—a smile!

Sonnet.

The glorious star of morning would we blame
  Because it burns not on the front of night?
  Or the calm evening planet, that her light
Foretells not sunrise, with its herald-flame?
All things that are should subtly own the same
  Eternal law! the stars shine on aright,
  Each in its sphere; the souls of Love and Might
Their separate bounds of grace or grandeur claim;

Not on the low or lofty, great or small,
  Should justice fix for judgment; the true soul,
  Which sways its own world in serene control,
Highest or humblest—such the Master's call
  Shall summon upward, with its deep " well done,"
  And the just Father crown his faithful son!

Violets.

" Rare wine of flowers."—FLETCHER.

A gusty wind o'ersweeps the garden close,
And, where the jonquil, with the white-rod glows,
   Riots like some rude hoyden uncontrolled.
But here, where sunshine and coy shadows meet,
Out gleam the tender eyes of violets sweet,
   Touched by the vapory noontide's fleeting gold.

What subtlest perfume floats serenely up!
Ethereal wine that brims each delicate cup,
   Rifled by viewless Ariels of the air,
And lo! methinks from out these fairy flowers
Rise the strange shades of half forgotten hours,
   Pale, tearful, mute, and yet, O heaven, how fair!

Yea, fair and marvellous, gliding gently nigh,
Some with raised brows and eyes of constancy,
   Fixed with fond meanings on a goal above.
And some faint shades of weary, drooping grace,
Each with a nameless pathos on its face,
   Breathing of heart-break and sad death of love.

Slowly they vanish! while these odors steep
Spirit and sense, as if in waves of sleep,
   Mysterious and Lethean ; languid streams
Flowing through realms of twilight thought apart,
Whereon the half-closed petals of the heart
   Pulse flower-like o'er a whispering tide of
      dreams :—

Nor wakes the soul to outward sound or sight,
Till noonday beams declining, warm and light,
   A wood-breeze fans the dreamer's forehead calm;
Who feels as one long wrapped from pain and
      drouth,
By magic dreams dreamed in the fervid South,
   Beneath the golden shadows of the palm.

Whence?

Eërily the wind doth blow
 Through the woodland hollow;
Eërily forlorn and low,
 Tremulous echoes follow!

Whence the low wind's tortured plaint?
 Burden hopeless, dreary,
As the anguished tones that faint
 Down the *Miserere?*

Whence? From far-off seas its moan!
 Darksome waves and lonely,
Where the tempest, overblown,
 Leaves a death-calm only.

Thence it caught the awful cry
 Of some last pale swimmer,
O'er whose drowning brain and eye
 Life grows dim and dimmer—

Ere the billows claim their prey,
 Settling stern and lonely.

Where the storm-clouds, rolled away,
  Leave death-silence only!

So with pain the wind-heart sighs;
  Through its sad commotion
Weary sea-tides sob, and rise
  Wailing hints of Ocean!

Hist! oh hist! as spreads the mist,
  Wood and hill-slope doming,
By no grace of starlight kissed,
  'Mid the shadowy gloaming,

Drearier grows the wind, more drear
  Echoes shuddering follow,
Till a place of doom and fear
  Seems that haunted hollow!

Ariel.

———•◦•———

"My dainty Ariel."—TEMPEST.

————

A voice like the murmur of doves,
   Soft lightning from eyes of blue,
On her cheek a flush like Love's
   First delicate, rosebud hue;

Bright torrents of hazel hair,
   Which, glittering, flow and float
O'er the swell of her bosom fair,
   And the snows of her matchless throat;

Lithe limbs of a life so fine,
   That their rhythmical motion seems
But a part of the grace divine
   Of the music of haunted dreams;

Low, gurgling laughter, as sweet
   As the swallow's song i' the South,
And a ripple of dimples that, dancing, meet
   By the curves of a perfect mouth;

O creature of light and of air !
　O fairy sylph o' th' sun !
Hearts whelmed in the tidal gold of her hair
　Rejoice to be *so* undone !

The Cloud-star.

(A FABLE.)

Far up within the tranquil sky,
  Far up it shone;
Floating, how gently, silently,
  Floating alone!

A sunbeam touched its loftier side
  With deepening light;
Then to its inmost soul did glide,
  Divinely bright.

The Cloud, transfigured to a Star,
  Thro' all its frame
Throbbed in the fervent heavens afar—
  One pulse of flame:

One pulse of flame, which inward turned,
  And slowly fed
On its own heart, that burned, and burned,
  'Till almost dead,

The cloud, still imaged as a star,
    Waned up the sky;
Waned slowly, pallid, ghost-like, far,
    Wholly to die;

But die so grandly in the sun—
    The noonfire's breath—
Methinks the glorious death it won,
    Life! life! not death!

Meanwhile a million insect things
    Crawl on below,
And gaudy worms on fluttering wings
    Flit to and fro;

Blind to that cloud, which, grown a star,
    Divinely bright,
Waned in the deepening heavens afar,
    Till—lost in light!

Sonnet.

———•◦•———

As one who strays from out some shadowy glade,
Fronting a lur:d noontide, stern, yet bright,
O'er mart and tower, and castellated height,
Shrinks slowly backward, dazed and half afraid—
So I, whose household gods their stand have made
Far from the populous city's life and light,
Its roar of traffic and its stormy might,
Shrink as I pass beyond my woodland shade.

The wordly conflict, the tempestuous din
Of these vast capitals, on ear and brain
Beat with the loud, reiterated swell
Of one fierce strain of passion and of sin,
Strange as in nightmare dreams the mad refrain
Of some wild chorus of the vaults of Hell.

Sonnet.

Enough, this glimpse of splendor wed to shame;
Enough, this gilded misery, this bright woe.
Pause, genial Wind! that even here dost blow
Thy cheerful clarion; and from dust and flame
The noonday pest, the night-enshrouded blame,
Uplift and bear me where the wild flowers grow
By many a golden dell-side sweet and low,
Shrined in the sylvan Eden whence I came.

O woodland water! O fair-whispering pine!
Loved of the dryad none but I have viewed!
O dew-lit glen, and lone glade, breathing balm,
Receive and bless me, till this tumult rude
Merged in your verdant solitudes divine,
My soul once more hath found her ancient calm!

Sweetheart, Good-Bye!

A SONG.

Sweetheart, good-bye! Our varied day
Is closing into twilight gray,
And up from bare, bleak wastes of sea
The north-wind rises mournfully;
A solemn prescience, strangely drear,
Doth haunt the shuddering twilight air;
It fills the earth, it chills the sky—
　　Sweetheart, good-bye!

Sweetheart, good-bye! Our joys are passed,
And night with silence comes at last;
All things must end—yea, even love—
Nor know we, if reborn above,
The heart-blooms of our earthly prime
Shall flower beyond these bounds of time.
" Ah! death alone is sure!" we cry—
　　Sweetheart, good-bye!

Sweetheart, good-bye! Through mist and tears
Pass the pale phantoms of our years,

Once bright with spring, or subtly strong
When summer's noontide thrilled with song ;
Now wan, wild-eyed, forlornly bowed,
Each rayless as an autumn cloud
Fading on dull September's sky—
    Sweetheart, good-bye!

Sweetheart, good-bye! The vapors rolled
Athwart yon distant, darkening wold,
Are types of what our world doth know
Of tenderest loves of long ago ;
And thus, when all is done and said,
Our life lived out, *our* passion dead,
What can their wavering record be
But tinted mists of memory ?
Oh! clasp and kiss me ere we die—
    Sweetheart, good-bye!

Sonnet.

The winds are loud and trumpet-clear to-day;
   They seem to sound an onset, half in ire,
   Half in the wildness of a vague desire
To force Spring's fairy vanguard to delay;
For here, methinks, worn winter stands at bay—
   Yet stands how vainly! spring-time's subtlest fire
   Melts his cold heart to nothingness, while nigher
Draw April hosts, and rearward powers of May—

All maiden verdures, concords of sweet air,
   Stealing as dawn steals gently on the world;
   Breezes, balm-laden, blown from distant seas,
With armies of blush-roses, dew-impearled—
Till Earth reclaimed from Winter's grim despair
   Blooms as once bloomed the fair Hesperides.

Frida and her Poet.

A brave young Poet, born in days of Eld,
Dwelt 'mid the frozen Northlands; he beheld,
And wondering, sung the marvels of the Ice,
The swirl of snow-flakes, and the quaint device
Wrought on the fir-trees by the glittering sleet;
And loved on stormy heights, cloud-girt, to greet
The gray ger-falcon towering o'er the sea;
To watch the waves, and mark the cloud-drifts flee,
Big with the wrath of tempests; yet, his heart,
Soft as the inner rose-leaves of the Spring,

Rich with young life, and love's sweet blossoming.
Too soon, alas! from life and love did part:
Veiled was the fate that smote him; unaware
What sudden, blasting doom had drawn so near,
A strange blight breathed upon him, and—he died!

On earth to die, in heaven be glorified,—
Such was the Minstrel's portion; still he went
Through all the heavenly courts in discontent
And sombre grief, the pathos of his woe
Rising at times to such wild overflow

As forced its wailful utterance into song.
That passionate rush of music, the heart's wrong
Set to the sweetness of harmonious chords,
The All-Father, Odin, o'er the clash of swords,
And din of heroes feasting at the boards
Of loud Valhalla, heard: thereon he sought
This lonely soul, in highest heaven o'erfraught
With mortal memories. "Wherefore lift'st thou
    here,"
The All-Father asked, "these measures of despair?"
"Because my mortal Love," the Poet said,
"With time grows gray and wrinkled; on her head,
So golden bright in youth's benignant prime,
Chill frosts of age have left their hoary rime;
Her eyes are dimmed, her soft cheeks' rosy red
Hath with the flowers of many a spring-tide fled;
And so when Heaven shall claim her—ah! the
    pain!—
I shall not know mine earthly love again!"

To whom the God, "But doth she love thee still?"
"Her love, like mine, nor years, nor change can
    kill,"
The Minstrel answered: "Faith, a ceaseless shower,
Keeps fair and bright our love's immaculate flower."

" I loose thy heavenly bonds,—I bid thee go !"
The All-Father cried, " and seek thy Love below!"
To earth he came: drear waste and flowery lea
Beheld his search 'mid fettered folk and free;
Yet all his toils but brought the direful stress
Of lone heart-yearning, grief, and weariness,
Till hope died out, and all his soul was dark.

At last, when aimless as an autumn leaf
Borne on November's idle winds afar,
He roamed a sea-beach wild, by moon or star
Unlighted, in his dreariest hour of grief
And desolate longing, on his eyes a spark
Of tiny radiance through the clouded night
Flashed from a cottage window on a height,
Next the dim billows of the moaning main.

There broke a sudden lightning on his brain
Of prescient expectation,—then, before
Its glow could fade, he trod the cottage floor,
And saw in tattered raiment, wan and dead,
An ancient withered woman on a bed,
Of whom a crone, as shrunk almost as she,
Said, with drawn lips, and blinking wearily,
" Lo ! here thine old Love !   Hast thou come so far
To find how cares may blight us, death may mar ?"

As ebbs a flood-tide, so his eager breath
Sank slowly. "Oh, the awful front of death!"
He moaned. "Yet wherefore shudder? Thou, my
    Love,
Art precious still; nor shalt thou move above,
An alien soul, albeit no longer fleet,
Nor fair, thou roam'st through Heaven with totter-
    ing feet,
Bent, aged form, and face bedimmed by tears;
I only ask to *know* thee, while the years
Eternal roll!"

      He bids a last farewell
To this world's life, again prepared to dwell
On heights celestial, in whose golden airs
The heart, at least, shall shed earth's wintry cares,
And blooming, breathe the vernal heats of Heaven.

Twice ransomed soul! thou spirit that has striven
With countless ills, and conquered all thy foes,
Rise with the might of morning, the repose
Of moonlit night, and entering Heaven once more—
Behold! who first doth meet thee by the door,
With smiling brow, and gently parted lips,
And eyes wherein no vestige of eclipse

From pain, or death, or any evil thing,
Lies darkly, but whose passionate triumphing,
In peace attained, and true love crowned at last,
Hath such rare joy and sweetness round her cast,
She seems an Angel on the heights of bliss.
And yet a mortal maid 'twere heaven to kiss!

To whom the Singer, in a voice that seems
Vague, and half-muffled in the mist of dreams:—
"Art thou the little Frida that I knew
So long—ah! long ago? Thine eyes are blue,
Deep blue like hers, and brimmed with tender dew,
Through which love's starlight smiles—art thou, in
　　sooth,
The sweet, true-hearted Frida of my youth?"

She drew more closely to the Poet's side,
And nestling her small hand in his, replied,
As half in tremulous wonder, half delight:—
"I *am* thy little Frida, in thy sight
Fair once, and well beloved—Ah me! ah me!
Hast thou forgotten?" "Nay; but whose" (quoth
　　he,)
"Yon withered corse, on which I gazed below,
With pale shrunk limbs, and furrowed face of woe?

Thy corse, *thy* face, they told me!"   " Yea, but
    know,
O Love! that earth, and things of earth, are passed:
That here, where, soul to soul, we meet at last,
The merciful Gods have made this wise decree :—
Love, in Heaven's tongue, means immortality
Of youth and joy; then, wheresoe'er we go,
Loving and loved through these high courts divine,
Mine eyes eternal youth shall drink from thine;
And thou forevermore shalt find in me
The tender maid who walked the world with thee,
Thy little Frida, loved so long ago!"

In the Bower.

The gusty and passionate March hath died;
And now in the golden April-tide
There sits in the shade of her jasmine bower
A maid more fair than an April flower.

The delicate curve of her perfect mouth,
Whose tints grow warm in the fervid South,
She stoops to press, as she murmurs low,
On a note upraised in her hand of snow.

What words are writ on the tiny scroll?
What thoughts lie deep in the maiden's soul?
Oh, is it with bliss of her love she sighs?
Is the light but Love's in those shy brown eyes?

So thinks the mock-bird trilling his lay
On the tremulous top of the lilac spray;
He views the maid, on his perch apart,
And his song is meant for her secret heart.

So thinks the breeze, for its frolic free
With the rose's stem, and the wing o' the bee

It leaves, to sigh in the maiden's ear,
"He is coming, sweet! he is almost here!"

So thinks the sun, for his ardent beams,
Grown mellow and soft as a virgin's dreams,
Through the vine-leaf shadows steal coyly down,
And she wears his light like a bridal crown.

Let the songster trill, and the breezes sigh,
And the sun weave crowns of his light i' the sky;
She heeds them not, for a step is heard,
And her soul leaps up like a startled bird—

Her soul leaps up, but it is not fear:
He is coming, sweet! he is here! is here!
And she flies to his bosom, (ah! panting dove,)
And is folded home on the heart of love!

Sonnet.

TO ——

Fair Muse, beloved of all, thou art no high
Imperious goddess of the mount or main,
But a sweet maiden of the pastoral plain,
To whom the hum of bees, the west wind's sigh,
The lapse of waters murmuring tranquilly,
Come, like soft music of a May-tide dream.
Yet, times there are when some imperial THEME,
Born of a stormy sunset's marvellous sky,
And heralded by thunder and fierce flame,
Sweeps o'er thy vision with a mien sublime,
And mighty voices, calling on thy name:
Then dost thou rise, exultant, thrilled, inspired,
Thy song a clarion lay that stirs our time,
Hot from the soul some secret God hath fired!

Lucifer's Deputy.

A MEDIÆVAL LEGEND.

A Poet once, whose tuneful soul, perchance,
Too fondly leaned toward sin, and sin's romance,
On a long vanished eve, so calm and clear
None could have deemed an evil spirit near,
Brooding ill deeds, was summoned by a writ,
In the due form of Hades, to the Pit;
A red-nosed, red-haired fiend the summoner,
About whose horrent head his locks did stir
Like half-waked serpents! "Well," in wrath and
    woe,
The Poet cried, "whom the De'il drives *must* go,
Whate'er the goal! Yet much I wish that he
Had sent as guide some nobler fiend than thee,
Thou hideous varlet!"
      "Come, keep cool, I say,"
Counseled the other sagely, "while *you may !*"
Whereon, as half in scorn and half in ire,
He haled the Poet to the realm of fire.

Arrived in bounds Hadéan, a vast rout
Of fiends they met, who rushed tumultuous out,
To roam the earth and those doomed spirits snare
Who unsuspecting lived and acted there;
Till in a few brief seconds the whole crew
Of crowding demons—black, brown, green and blue—
All but their haughty chief, his form upreared
Through the red mist, had wildly disappeared.
Then said the dark archangel to the bard:
" Thine eye is bright, thou hast a shrewd regard;
And, therefore, ere I likewise o'er the marge
Of Hades wing my way for some brief hours,
To thee I choose to delegate my powers
As chief and sovereign of this kingdom dread,
The which, if well thou guardest, by my head
Thy recompense, when I come back, shall be
A luscious tid-bit, garnished daintily—
No meaner *entrée* than a roasted monk,
(Before he's cooked we'll make the rascal drunk,
To spice his juices !) ; or, if thou'dst prefer
Yon leaner and less succulent usurer,
Why, of our toil and time with trifling loss,
We'll serve *him* up, larded with golden sauce !"

But while the absent fiends their cunning tasked

To trap unwary souls, thick cloaked and masked,
One entered Hades who did soon entice
The heedless bard to play a game at dice,
Staking the souls he held in charge thereon.
The stranger played superbly—played, and won.
So, gathering round him the freed souls, with care
And kind despatch, safe to the outward air
He led them triumphing ; and all who now
Looked on his unmasked face and glorious brow
Knew that St. Peter stood amongst them there.

But when the devils, trooping homeward, found
Their kingdom void—its conflagrations drowned
As 'twere by showers from Heaven—such curses
    rose—
Like thunder bellowing through the strange repose
Which late had reigned—the Poet's head whirled
    round,
Stunned by the tumult. But ere long, with whirr
And furious whizz, his right hand Lucifer
Brought in such stinging contact with one cheek
And then the other, that our minstrel, weak
From pain and fear, sank trembling on the floor.
But sternly Satan pointed to the door,
Wherethrough his faithless guard, with many a kick

And echoing thump, and one swift merciless prick
Of a keen pitchfork, was thrust forth in shame
From out the empire of fierce grief and flame,
In even more woeful plight than when he came!
Then Lucifer upraised his arms and swore
A mighty oath that Hades' lurid door
No Poet's form should ever enter more!

So, brother bards, whate'er ye write or do,
Be fearless.   Hades holds no place for you:
Since if on earth men deem your worth but small,
Why there, 'tis plain, ye have no worth at all!

Preëxistence.

—•••—

While sauntering through the crowded street,
Some half-remembered face I meet,

Albeit upon no mortal shore
That face, methinks, hath smiled before.

Lost in a gay and festal throng,
I tremble at some tender song—

Set to an air whose golden bars
I must have heard in other stars.

In sacred aisles I pause to share
The blessings of a priestly prayer—

When the whole scene which greets mine eyes
In some strange mode I recognize

As one whose every mystic part
I feel prefigured in my heart.

At sunset, as I calmly stand,
A stranger on an alien strand—

Familiar as my childhood's home
Seems the long stretch of wave and foam.

One sails toward me o'er the bay,
And what he comes to do and say

I can foretell.   A prescient lore
Springs from some life outlived of yore.

O swift, instinctive, startling gleams
Of deep soul-knowledge! not as *dreams*

For aye ye vaguely dawn and die,
But oft with lightning certainty

Pierce through the dark, oblivious brain,
To make old thoughts and memories plain—

Thoughts which perchance must travel back
Across the wild, bewildering track

Of countless æons; memories far,
High-reaching as yon pallid star,

Unknown, scarce seen whose flickering grace
Faints on the outmost rings of space!

A Thousand Years from Now.

I sat within my tranquil room ;
   The twilight shadows sank and rose
With slowly flickering motions, waved
   Grotesquely through the dusk repose ;
There came a sudden thought to me,
   Which thrilled the spirit, flushed the brow—
A dream of what our world would be
   A thousand years from now !

If science on her heavenward search,
   Rolling the stellar charts apart,
Or delving hour by hour to win
   The secrets of earth's inmost heart—
If that her future apes her past,
   To what new marvels men must bow,
Marvels of land, and air, and sea,
   A thousand years from now !

If empires hold their wonted course,
   And blind republics will not stay
To count the cost of laws which lead
   Unerring to the State's decay—

What changes vast of realm and rule,
   The low upraised, the proud laid low,
Shall greet the unborn ages still,
   A thousand years from now!

Our creeds may change with mellowed times
   Of nobler hope, and love increased,
And some new Advent flood the world
   In glory from the haunted East—
While souls on loftier heights of faith
   May mark the mystic pathway grow
Clearer between their stand and heaven's,
   A thousand years from now!

These things *may be!* but what, perforce,
   Must with the ruthless epochs pass?
The millions' breath, the centuries' pomp,
   Sure as the wane of flowers or grass;
The earth so rich in tombs to-day,
   There scarce seems space for death to sow,
Who, who shall count her churchyard wealth
   A thousand years from now?

And we—poor waifs! whose life-term seems,
   When matched with AFTER and BEFORE,
Brief as a summer wind's, or wave's
   Breaking its frail heart upon the shore,

We—human toys—that Fate sets up
 To smite, or spare—I marvel how
These souls shall fare, in what strange sphere,
 A thousand years from now?

Too vague, too faint for mortal ken
 That far, phantasmal Future lies;
But sweet! one sacred truth I read,
 Just kindling in your tear-dimmed eyes,
That States may rise, and States may set,
 With age earth's tottering pillars bow,
But hearts like ours can ne'er forget,
 And though we know not *where*, nor *how*,
Our conscious love shall blossom yet,
 A thousand years from now!

Sonnet.

I stood in twilight by the winter's sea;
The spectral tides with hollow, hungry roar,
Broke massed and mighty on the shrinking shore.
The sea birds wailed; the foam flew wild and free.
Ruthless as fate, upborne victoriously,
A fierce wind clove the billows urged afar
With vengeful rhythm toward the western star,
Just risen beyond a gaunt, grey cypress tree.

Then twilight waned in cloud-descending night,
The sole star died, as if some phantom hand
Wiped out its radiance; in the void profound
The wind and waters (blended in one sound,
Awful, mysterious,) with invisible might
Thrilled the blank heavens, and smote the affrighted
    strand!

When All has been Said and Done.

TO RICHARD HENRY STODDARD,

(In reply to his poem called "*Wishing and Having.*")

> "Perhaps it will all come right at last;
>   It may be, when all is done,
> We shall be together in some good world,
>   Where to *wish* and to *have* are one."—STODDARD.

O Friend! be sure that a spirit came,
    In the gloom of your saddened hour,
To plant that hope in your hopeless heart,
    Like the seed of an Eden flower.
The seed may rest in your brooding breast,
    Half stifled in cold and night,
Or be only felt as a yearning dim
    Toward comforting peace and light;
But 'twill burst, some day, into perfect bloom,
    And fruition be brightly won;
For the earth-life fades like a dream o' the dark
    When all has been said and done!

The earth-life fades in its sin and pain;
    But whatever of sweet and pure,

Breathed over its pallor and flushed its gloom,
    Surviveth for evermore.
O, not as the ghost of a mortal joy,
    But as Joy herself from the dead
Upraised to the clear, calm courts of Heaven,
    With a halo around her head;
'Tis only the vile and the sad shall die
    With the wane of an earthly sun,
And pass like a vision as man awakes
    When all has been said and done!

Do you think you have lost your days for aye
    In the heart of the woods of spring,
By that seaside town that is glimpsed through mist,
    Like the white of a petrel's wing?
Do you think that the patter of tiny feet
    Shall never come back again,
And that those whom the rage of Death had killed
    Are in sooth forever slain?
Look up! look up! as the Hope commands,
    From the ruth of the angels won;
The earth-woe fades like a dream o' the night,
    When all has been said and done!

O God, we wander in devious ways,
    Till the end comes, stern and stark;

We lift our voices of useless wail
    From the depths of the hollow Dark;
Yet the Christ is there, though we see him not,
    But only when sorrow lowers
Wildest, we feel through the hollow Dark
    A strange, warm hand in ours;
And a voice is heard in the music of Heaven,
    Saying: " Courage and hope, O, son !"
The earth-woe fades like a dream o' the night,
    When all has been said and done !

On the Death of Canon Kingsley.

Mortals there are who seem, all over, flame,
Vitalized radiance, keen, intense, and high,
Whose souls, like planets in a dominant sky,
Burn with full forces of eternity:

Such was his soul, and such the light which came
From that pure heaven he lived in; holiest worth
Of will and work was his, to brighten earth,
Heal its foul wounds, and beautify its dearth.

He dwelt in clear white purity apart,
Yet walked the world; through many a sufferer's
　　door
He shone like morning; comfort streamed before
His footsteps; on the feeble and the poor

He lavished the rich spikenard of his heart.
Christ's soldier! to His trumpet-call he sprung,
Eager, elate; valiant of pen and tongue,
Grand were the words he spake, the songs he sung.

Still, hero-priest! born out of thy due time—
Thou should'st have lived when on thine England's
　　sod

Giants of faith and seers of freedom trod,
Daring all things to break the oppressor's rod.

Great in thine own age, thou had'st been sublime
In theirs—that age of fervent, fruitful breath,
When, scorning treachery, and defying death,
Her true knights girt their loved Elizabeth,

Seeing on her the centuries' hopes were set;
Then hadst thou ranged with Raleigh land and sea,
Bible and sword in hand, gone forth with Leigh,
The tyrant smote, the heathen folk made free!

Yea! but to God and grace thou hast paid thy
    debt,
In measure scarce less glorious and complete
Than theirs who bearded on his chosen seat
The bloody Antichrist; or, fleet to fleet,

Thundered through storms of battle-wrack and fire
At Britain's Salamis;* the heroic strain
Ran purpling all thy nature like a vein
Oped from God's heart to thine; the loftiest plane

Of thought and action, purpose and desire
Thou trod'st on triumphing; thy Viking's face

* Alluding to the defeat of the " Invincible Armada."

Showed granite-willed, yet softened into grace
By effluence of good deeds, the angelic race
Of prayers to prompt and aid them! Fare thee
    well,
Clear spirit and strong! thy life-work nobly done,
Shines beautiful as some unsetting sun
O'er Arctic summers; chords of victory run
Even through the mournful boom of thy deep
    funeral knell!

Thunder at Midnight.

At midnight wakening, through my startled brain
The sudden thunder crashed a chord of pain;

I rose, and, awe-struck, hearkened! overhead
In one long, loud, reverberant peal of dread,

Ceaseless it rolled, till as a sea of fire,
The climax gained, must wave by wave retire;

So, half reluctant, up the heights of space
The refluent thunder softened into grace,

Its deep, harsh menace changed to murmurs low
As the lost south wind's, muffled in the snow;

Waning through whisperous echoes less and less,
Till the last echo sleeps in gentleness.

Thus 'minded am I of that Law of Old
Which down the slopes of awful Sinai rolled,

Smote men with judgment terrors; yet, at last,
The lightning flame and mystic tumult passed,

Lapsed down the ages, echoing less and less
Jehovah's wrath, till, changed to tenderness,

The vengeful Law, which once man's faith sufficed,
Melts into mercy on the heart of CHRIST!

The Arctic Visitation.

Some air-born genius, with malignant mouth,
Breathed on the cold clouds of an Arctic zone—
Which o'er long wastes of shore and ocean blown
Swept threatening, vast, toward the amazéd South:

Over the land's fair form at first there stole
A vanward host of vapors, wild and white;
Then loomed the main cloud cohorts, massed in
     might,
Till earth lay corpse-like, reft of light and soul;

Death-wan she lay, 'neath heavens as cold and pale;
All nature drooped toward darkness and despair;
The dreary woodlands, and the ominous air
Were strangely haunted by a voice of wail.

The woeful sky slow passionless tears did weep,
Each shivering rain-drop frozen ere it fell;
The woodman's axe rang like a muffled knell;
Faintly the echoes answered, fraught with sleep.

The dawn seemed eve; noon, dawn eclipsed of
     grace;

The evening, night; and tender night became
A formless void, through which no starry flame
Touched the veiled splendor of her sorrowful face:

Like mourning nuns, sad-robed, funereal, bowed,
Day followed day; the birds their quavering notes
Piped here and there from feeble, querulous throats.
Fierce cold beneath—above, one riftless cloud

Wrapped the mute world—for now all winds had
    died—
And, locked in ice, the fettered forests gave
No sign of life; as silent as the grave
Gloomed the dim, desolate landscape far and wide.

Gazing on these, from out the mist one day
I saw, a shadow on the shadowy sky,—
What seemed a phantom bird, that, faltering nigh,
Perched by the roof-tree on a withered spray;

With drooping breast he stood, and drooping head;
This fateful time had wrought the minstrel wrong;
Even as I gazed, our Southland lord of song
Dropped through the blasted branches, breathless,
    dead!

Yet chillier grew the gray, world-haunting shade,

.Through which, methought, quick, tremulous wings
were heard;

Was it the ghost of that heartbroken bird

Bound for a land where sunlight cannot fade?

The Vision in the Valley.

———•••———

Amid the loveliest of all lonely vales,
  Couched in soft silences of mountain calm,
  And broadly shadowed both by pine and palm,
O'er which a tremulous golden vapor sails
Forever, though unbreathed on by a breeze
  Or any wind of heaven, serenely sleeps
  A lucid fountain, from whose fathomless deeps
Come murmurs stranger than the twilight sea's.

That golden vapor, buoyed without a breath,
  Tints to its own fair bloom the limpid tide,
Through which erewhile the solemn vision rose
  Of a calm face, benignly glorified
By all we dream or yearn for of pure rest—
Profound, Lethéan, passionless repose.
  Still through the silence mystic murmurs sighed,
Fraught with far meanings, vague and unexpressed,
  Till at the last, upbreathing, weird and near,
  The voice of that pale phantom thrilled mine
    ear—
"*Behold the face, the marvellous face, of* DEATH *!*"

The Wind of Onset.

With potent north winds rushing swiftly down,
Blended in glorious chant, on yesternight
Old Winter came with locks and beard of white,
    The hoarfrost glittering on his ancient crown :

He sent his icy breathings through the pane,
He raved and rattled at the close shut doors,
Then waned with hollow murmur down the moors,
    To rise, revive and sweep the world again.

The chorus of great winds which gird him round
Hold many voices—the deep trumpet's swell,
The air harp's mournful burden of farewell,
    The fife's shrill tones, the clarion's silvery sound :

But o'er the roof-tree, 'round the gable rings
Loudest his WIND OF ONSET, hour by hour,
Till a new sense of almost rapturous power
    Comes on the mighty waftage of his wings;

Sense of fresh hope and faith's rekindled glow,
The awakened aim, the brain drawn tense and
      high,

To shoot its fiery thoughts against the sky,
   Like arrows launched from some deft archer's
      bow !

All latent forces of our being start
To marshalled order, ranged in battle line,
While the roused life-blood with a thrill divine
   Runs tingling thro' the chambers of the heart.

Summer is rich with dreams of languid tone;
October sunsets feed the soul with light;
But give *me* winter's war wind in his might,
   O'er the scourged lands and turbulent oceans
      blown.

The Visit of Mahmoud Ben Suleim to Paradise.

---•◆•---

Beneath the shadow of a breezeless palm
Mahmoud Ben Suleim, in the evening calm,
Sat, with his gravely meditative eyes
Turned on the waning wonder of the skies;
What time beside him paused a brother sage,
Whose flowing locks, like his, were white with age:
His gaze, a half-veiled fire, seemed sadly cast
Inward, to scan the records of his past—
Perchance the Past of Man—and thence to draw
From far experience, sanctified by awe
Of God's mysterious ways, some hint to tell
Who of the dead in Heaven and who in Hell
Dwelt now in endless bliss or endless bale.

Thus, while he mused, the old man's face grew pale
With stringent memories; on his laboring thought
Vague speculations, dim and doubtful wrought
From out the fragments of the vanished years.
At length he said: "Ben Suleim, lend thine ears
To that I fain would ask thee.   Thou art wise

In sacred lore, in pure philosophies;
So tell me now thine inmost thought of Heaven
And Heaven's fair habitants."

      " Whoe'er hath striven,"
Ben Suleim answered, "to the extremest verge
Of spiritual power, across death's dreary surge
Hath passed, to find the fathomless peace of God!"

" Yea," quoth the other, smiting on the sod
His staff, impatiently. " I know! I know!
But who of all *we* have seen or loved below
Think'st thou in Aidenn?"

       Slowly from his lips,
Wrapped by the smoke-wreaths in a half-eclipse,
Ben Suleim's pipe was lowered: "My friend," said
  he,
" Hark to this vision of eternity,
Which in the long-gone time of youth did seem
To rise before me in a twilight dream.
Methought the life on earth had passed away,
That near me spread the new, immortal day
Of Paradise; but yet mine eyes looked back
On this our clouded world, and marked the track
My waning life-course still left glimmering there.
Behold! all dues of funeral dole and prayer

Mine heirs had paid me; through the cypress gloom
I saw the glitter of my new-made tomb,
Whereon so many a blazoned virtue shone,
A blush seemed gathering o'er the hardened stone,
And I, albeit a spirit, flushed with shame.
Nathless, just then to Eden gates I came,
And, at the outmost wicket thundering loud,
Summoned full soon an angel from the cloud
Which girds those heavenly portals, blent with mist
Of shifting rainbow arcs of amethyst,
Who, somewhat harshly for an angel, said
I knocked as if an hundred thousand dead,
Not *one* poor soul, besieged the heavenly door.
He raised his luminous hands, which hovered o'er
For a brief moment, like a flash of stars,
The sapphire brilliance of the circling bars,
Then one by one unclosed them.   Entered in
The Realm celestial, safe from pain and sin,
I, stretched at ease, with shadows cool and dim
Floating about me, thus did question him :
' Fair Seraph, speak.   Is not this Land Divine,
Rife with pure souls, once faithful friends of mine?'
'Nay! be content if, wandering here and there,
Thou meet'st a *few*—none in the loftiest sphere.'
' Where, then,' I cried, ' is holy Ibn Becár?

If not the highest he, surely not far
Beneath the highest that clear spirit beams?'
'Ah! thou art muffled still in earthly dreams,'
The angel answered.   'If on *him* thou'dst call,
Pass downward, for he's not in Heaven at all!'
'Dread Allah! can it be? So just a man
Walked not, methought, the streets of Ispahan.
Morn after morn, year after year his feet,
Alike in summer's bloom and winter's sleet,
Bore him to worship in the sacred place.
What righteous zeal burned hotly in his face!
And when inspired his heavenly vows he made,
Or 'neath the innermost mosque devoutly prayed,
Why, even the roaring Dervish, robed and cowled,
Shrunk from those pious lungs, which almost
      howled
Creation deaf.   A saint we deemed him—one
Pure as the snow, yet ardent as the sun—
Who, not content with turning toward the light
His own blest feet, must set on paths of right
All erring brethren!' 'True,' the angel cried;
'But Ibn Becár, down to the day he died,
Kept on his neighbor's ways so keen an eye
He lost at length his own straight course thereby;
And, though the purblind World hath guessed it
      not,

He bides in Eblis' Kingdom; fierce and hot
The waves of Hades róll above him now.'
Amazed, I bowed my head, just whispering low
An '*Allah Kebur.*' Next: ' How fares it, then,'
I asked, ' with Hafiz, the wise scribe, whose pen
Signed many a deed of gift, and scored his name
High on the roll of charitable hearts?'
Clear came the answer: ''Mid thy public marts
No soul more sordid strove with Heaven to drive
Its wicked bargains.   Largely would he give
To general charities; but, sooth to say,
Whene'er he 'scaped the broad, bright gaze of Day
He stamped with cruel heel the writhing poor,
Would turn the perishing beggar from his door,
And wring from friendless widows the last crust
Saved for their half-starved children.   God is just;
So Hafiz dwells not here.'
     In faltering tone,
As dropped from one who deals with things un-
 known,
I questioned next: 'Abdallah, *he* is saved?'
'Nay; for, albeit with *seeming* truth he braved
Temptation, and each wise and sacred saw,
Wrought from the precepts of our prophet's law,
Fell soft as Hybla's honey from his mouth,

Yet his whole nature withered in the drouth
Of drear hypocrisy.   By stealth he bought
Strong waters of the Giaour, and nightly sought
Oblivion from sweet opiates of the South.
Sickness he feigned, to gain in these his cure;
And once, that he might tipple more and more,
Moved to a province rife with serpents dread,
Because, by such as knew his wiles, 'twas said
He drank the poison of each treacherous throat,
To seek in fiery wine an antidote.
Nathless, a serpent slew him and his home
Is far from ours.'

                    My thoughts began to roam
Vaguely, in loose disorder.   Yet again:
'What of Kalkarri, he whose songs of pain
And joy alike forever struck the key,
The under-note of golden purity,
Virtue his theme and heavenly love his muse?'
'Thou fool and blind!   Kalkarri could not choose
But sing mellifluous verses; yet in him
The light of truth was always blurred and dim.
A tireless trick of tinkling rhymes he had,
And nought he cared what spirit, good or bad,
O'erruled his lay.   The good, perchance, *paid* best;
Therefore he sang of heavenly joy and rest,

But sang of that whereof he shall not taste.'
' Just Allah !' sighed I, ' see what barren waste
Drinks up my hopes.   Since none of all I named
Here for the sacred roll hath Allah claimed,
I pray thee tell me *whom* his will hath blessed.'
' Dost thou remember S a ä d i ?' ' What, that
    wretch
Who shod the Bactrian camels—who would fetch
Strange oaths from far to sow our wholesome air
With moral poison ?' ' True, the man did swear,'
Confessed the Bright One, sadly. ' Yet so strong
His penitent sorrow o'er the hateful wrong
Done his own soul and Allah, and so rife
With tireless effort his whole earnest life
To smite the giant tempters in his soul—
To kill them outright, or with firm control
Hold them in native darkness chained and cowed—
At last he conquered, and our Lord allowed
His weary soul to quaff the founts of balm.'

Amazement held me dumb.   Within the palm
Waving above, just then a whispering breeze
Rose, and passed up the long-ranked, radiant trees
Which lined the hills of Heaven.   It seemed a sigh
Born of soft Mercy's immortality,

Wafted toward the throne! The Bright One then,
Lifting his voice harmonious, spake again :
' Ferdusi, the small merchant by the Quays,
Too poor to give, but with a heart as broad
As the broad sky, reverent of faith and God;
Islal-ed-Din, who, though he could not make
The commonest prayer, would yet exclaim Amen !
To those who did, so warmly, for the sake
Of truth and fervent worship, all might see
His generous spirit's large sincerity—
Both *these* are with us.'

      ' But, Wassaf,' said I,
The blameless teacher, who methinks came nigh
Virtue as pure as frail humanity
On earth may compass ?' ' Yea; his soul *is* here,
But his soul wanders in the humblest sphere.
For, mark thee, though no damning sin did stain
This Wassaf's record, still in blood and brain
So weak was he, his pale life-currents flowed
So like dull streamlets through a wan abode
Of windless deserts, that he lived and died
Ne'er by a sharp temptation terrified;
And if his course the Prophet's law fulfilled,
And near his path all passionate gusts were
  stilled,

What credit to him?   His to coldly live,
Act, fade—a creature tamely negative.
But lo! in flaming contrast the hot stir
Of Agha's fate—Agha, the flute player—
Glutton on earth, wine-bibber, and the rest,
He still is held in Heaven a nobler guest
Than all your Wassafs—proper, crimeless, cool,
And soulless, almost, as a stagnant pool.
For Agha's blood a furious torrent ran;
Half brutal he, half tiger and half man,
In health and power, the body's lustful force,
Whose strength to fetter in its turbulent course
Had taxed an angel's will.   His nature sore
Tormented him; yet o'er and o'er and o'er
From some vast fall he lifted prayerful eyes,
And like a Titan strove to *storm* the skies,
Which, through unequalled strife and travails passed,
His hero-soul hath grandly won at last!

No more! no more!' the glorious Presence said.
' In light to come thy knowledge perfected
Shall bloom in flower and fruit; but, Suleim, say,
Hast thou beheld the swift sky-rocket's ray
Burn up the heavens?   How beautiful at first
Its splendors gleamed, too soon, alas! to burst

And die in outer darkness!   Thus it is
With many a soul, soaring, men dream, to bliss.
Awhile they mount, clear, dazzling, drunk with
    light,
To sink in ruin and the desolate night.
Would'st know the true believer?   *He* is one
Whose faith in deeds shines perfect as the sun.
His soul, a shaft feathered by works of grace,
Death, the grim archer, launches forth in space ;
It cleaves the clouds, o'ershoots the vaporous wall
That waves 'twixt earth and heaven its mystic pall,
To light, at last, unerring, strong and fleet,
In the deep calm which lies at Allah's feet !" "

My Daughter.

Thou hast thy mother's eyes, my child—
Her deep dark eyes: the undefiled
Sweetness which breathes around her mouth,
A perfect rosebud of the south,
And the broad brow, as smooth to-day
As when in life's auspicious May
I clasped her to an ardent breast
With yearnings of divine unrest.

Thou hast thy mother's voice, as low
And soft as happy winds that blow
At springtime o'er the wild-bloom beds,
When the blue harebells lift their heads
To hearken to those strains of peace,
And through the lustrous day's decease
Drink in the sunset-beams that float
Downward from glittering airs remote.

Thou hast thy mother's heart, no less
Than all her body's loveliness—
A heart as firmly brave and true,
O'er-brimming now with morning dew

Of hopeful light as doth a flower;
Yet strong to meet misfortune's hour,
And for the sake of loving ruth
Lie down and perish in its youth.

Child! child! so fair, so good thou art,
Sometimes an awful pang my heart
Pierces as thus I gaze on thee.
Too rare a thing thou seem'st to be
Long in this barren world to smile;
Methinks, with many a heavenly wile,
Unseen, but felt, the angels stray
Near thee, to tempt thy soul away.

Oh! heed them not. Why should they cull
My one sweet blossom? Heaven is full
Of just such spirits. Leave her here,
Kind seraphs! our poor joys to share,
Our griefs to brighten by her love;
Pass on to your calm homes above,
And thus in mercy spare to earth
The angel of my heart and hearth.

'Tis strange, but yet so fresh and whole,
So radiant in my brain and soul

Doth this enchanting image dwell,
This pure, unrivaled miracle
Of maidenhood and modest grace,
I vow that I behold her face,
Hear her low tones, and mark her mien,
So gentle, virginal, serene,   .

Clearly, as if her voice and brow,
In softest sooth, beguiled me now ;
As if, incarnate and benign,
She placed her little hand in mine,
And her long midnight tresses rare
Were mingling with my snow-touched hair.
And yet she only lives for me
In golden realms of fantasie,
A creature born of air and beam,
The delicate darling of a dream.

Our " Humming Bird."

Ah, well I know the reason why
They called her by that graceful name :
She seems a creature born with wings,
O'er which a rainbow spirit flings
Fair hues of softly shifting flame ;
Light is she as the changeful air,
Borne on gay humors everywhere,
           Bewitchingly.

Her soul hath seldom breathed a sigh ;
No hint of care hath ever stirred
Her being; sunshine and the breeze
Have been the fairy witnesses
Of all those joys our happy bird
Hath from the golden fountains drawn
Of youth unsullied as the dawn,
           So lavishly.

Full many a flower, just hovering nigh,
In life's broad garden, rife with sweets,
She deftly drains of nectar dew ;
Then, sylph-like, sweeps o'er pathways new

To taste some balmier bliss she meets;
Now flashing fast through myrtle bowers,
Now clinging to red lips of flowers,
                    Capriciously.

Forbear, rash heart! forbear to try
Our bird to capture with your wiles,
For, lo! she glimmers like a beam
Of fancy, on from dream to dream;
Vain are a lover's tears or smiles
To check her flight bewildering,
To tame her soul, or chain her wing
                    Submissively.

Nay! let the dazzling fairy fly
From flower to flower, so gladly whirled;
Cruel it were her matchless light
By one rude touch to dim or blight,
To see her luminous pinions furled
In grosser airs than those which stray
Round the fresh rose-buds of the May,
                    Deliciously.

Sonnet.

———•✦•———

Between the sunken sun and the fair moon
I stood, in fields through which a clear brook ran
With scarce perceptible motion; not a span
Of its smooth surface trembling to the tune
Of sunset breezes; " Ah ! delicious boon,"
I sighed, " of quiet; wise is Nature's plan,
Who in her realm, as in the soul of man,
Passes from storm to calm, from the loud noon

To dewy evening's soft and sacred lull :
Happy the heart that keeps its twilight hour,
And, in the depths of heavenly peace reclined,
Loves to commune with thoughts of tender power;
Thoughts that ascend—like angels beautiful—
A shining Jacob's ladder of the mind !"

Sonnet.

———•◆•———

Along the path thy bleeding feet have trod,
O, Christian mother! do the martyr-Years,
Patient in suffering, thro' the mist of tears
Uplift their brows thorn-circled unto God:
How bitterly our Father's chastening rod
Hath ruled within thy term of mortal days;
Yet in thy soul upspring the tones of praise
Freely as flowers from out a burial sod:

Nor hath a tireless faith essayed in vain
To win from sorrow that diviner rest
Which, like a sunset purpling thro' the rain
Of dying storms, maketh the darkness blest;
Grief is transfigured, and dethronèd Fears
Pale in the glory beckoning from the West.

www.ingramcontent.com/pod-product-compliance
Lightning Source LLC
Chambersburg PA
CBHW021126020726
47500CB00003B/937